Two Jews = Three Shuls

"A readable and engaging stew of murder mystery, synagogue politics (with which any reader engaged in their house of worship will chuckle with recognition and cringe with frustration), tensions over the role of women in Jewish religious life, and the impact of the Holocaust on the lives of survivors and their children. Tankoos has woven this together beautifully."

—DAVID SAPERSTEIN
Director Emeritus, Religious Action Center of Reform Judaism;
co-author of *Jewish Dimensions of Social Justice*

"Sandra Tankoos clearly understands the culture and moral code of those who choose to be active in synagogue life. The storyline is compelling, blending both mysticism and day-to-day reality, while struggling to find their rabbi's assassin. Recommended reading."

—MICHAEL WHITE
Senior Rabbi, Temple Sinai of Roslyn, Long Island

"This is a very smart book. It understands the language and culture of Jewish Long Island. It understands the inner workings—with all of the warts— of suburban synagogue life. Sides are drawn, irrationality hides behind faith, and petty jealousies abound . . . The reader cares about the search for the perpetrator of a dark deed. Mysticism meets love, and love unleashes memories of pain and of horrendous loss."

—STANLEY M. DAVIDS
Rabbi and Editor of *Deepening The Dialogue*

"So many issues that synagogues confront and don't confront—they are all in the story! And a murder to be solved as well! A real page-turner. A must-read for anyone and everyone who cares about religious life as it gets played out day to day."

—BENNETT MILLER
Rabbi Emeritus, Anshe Emeth Memorial Temple,
New Brunswick, New Jersey; National Chair, ARZA

"A Jewish whodunnit. Sandy Tankoos includes all the right Jewish elements of gossip, guilt, and ghosts (though Jewish law prohibits us from conjuring them up—but in this case it was the rabbi reaching out to his congregation's president.) There's even the prototypical Jewish mother . . . the rabbi's mother, who of course believes it was her daughter-in-law who killed her son. Can there be anything more Jewish and mysterious? This is truly a delightful read with wonderfully written Jewish characters that everyone can appreciate."

—ROBERT A. SILVERS
Senior Rabbi, Congregation B'nai Israel, Boca Raton, Florida

Two Jews = Three Shuls

SANDRA TANKOOS

Foreword by Josh Weinberg

RESOURCE *Publications* · Eugene, Oregon

Resource Publications
An Imprint of Wipf and Stock Publishers
199 W. 8th Ave., Suite 3
Eugene, OR 97401

www.wipfandstock.com

PAPERBACK ISBN: 978-1-7252-6794-7
HARDCOVER ISBN: 978-1-7252-6795-4
EBOOK ISBN: 978-1-7252-6796-1

Manufactured in the U.S.A.   06/03/20

To my grandchildren:
Samantha, Erica, Justin, Hudson, Aaron, and Mia
Always follow your dreams

Foreword

F ew people would have the courage to dive deep into some of the most challenging and difficult political arenas of synagogue politics. Many American Jews often wax nostalgic about the "good old days," when Jewish institutions thrived, ensconced in what seemed like the Golden Age for the suburban synagogue. Rabbis were larger than life and the changing and evolving American Jewry seemingly balanced out in the 1970's Conservative Movement. However, despite the success of institutions in what hindsight might offer to be their height, they were not without issues and anything but a serene or unified time.

American Jewish institutions have the power to bring people together, to raise significant funds in service of worthy causes, and serve as anchors for Jews seeking to find meaning and connection, education, and Jewish observance. But, like any institution or civilization, they also have the power to serve as the source of division, ideological indignation, and even great strife among their members and leaders.

Sandy Tankoos has offered her contribution and entered in the annals of modern/contemporary historical fiction with this impressive debut novel. Her life experience, having grown up in an activist and richly Jewish household filled with both Yiddishkeit and Zionism, keenly positions her to write this story, and her boundless creativity and imagination casts this as a synagogue-based whodunnit murder mystery, with none other than the revered rabbi as the central protagonist and victim.

Tankoos captures the congregational politics with real and vivid imagery, putting the reader straight into twentiteth-century American Jewish life. Having grown up in a rabbinic household, including a stint in a congregation-owned parsonage, I can attest to the authenticity in her voice, and the theatrics in which the unbridled imagination could lead to the tragic murder of a rabbi.

One of the central questions Tankoos's contribution raises is the question of evolution and adaptation to the changing times. As her character, Rabbi Levenson, digs in his heels over time, becoming stricter in his observance, more stringent in his outlook, and generally increasingly resistant to impending change, the up and coming generation is, at the same time, growing progressively impatient with their institution and its leaders. The message is clear that those who resist change, while they may not face the death penalty, will slowly fade into oblivion. Whether this surrounded the Conservative Movement's gradual inclusion and recognition of women and egalitarianism, acceptance of LGBTQ members of our community, or the questions and debates over inter-marriage in both the Reform and Conservative Movements today, we have seen a large swath change in our mainstream movements' approaches and a shift in policy. The tensions were great then, and in many ways remain so today along both political and ideological lines, and we can look to both the tragedy and reconciliation (no spoilers) of the people of Beth Torah as a caricature of our own lives and communities in order to learn our own lessons and parse out a resonating message for generations to come.

Tankoos has offered this volume, and in doing so has joined the field of some of the literary greats of Jewish-American literature who have contributed to this genre, brilliantly capturing the twentieth-century experience with their own twist of nuance and their own subtle-not-subtle critique. Philip Roth's *Goodbye Columbus*, with the famous and at-one-time controversial stories "The Conversion of the Jews" and "Eli the Fanatic," remains the all-time hero of this heyday. Saul Bellow and Bernard Malamud also mastered the genre, and other more contemporary authors such as Dara Horn, Nathan Englander, Jonathan Safran Foer, Nicole Kraus, Michael Chabon, Tova Mirvis, to name but a few, have shaped the kaleidoscopic view of American-Jewish life with their contributions, each with a unique voice and a penetrating message. As in Tankoos's novel, the Holocaust is like an uninvited guest whose presence is always felt and whose shadow is lurking in the background, just reminding everyone of its persistent and undeniable existence as a looming cloud in almost all American-Jewish fiction. In this book we also deeply feel the far-reaching ripples of the Holocaust on Jewish life, from the pathos of a survivor to the support-group-joining second generations of survivors. Tankoos forces us to reconcile with our past and to see if we might ever escape the throes of the greatest tragedy to befall our people in modern history. The cloud of the Holocaust could be interpreted as the underlying current that pushes us and guides and from which we will never escape—at least in the 20th century. Reflecting a quarter century after this novel is set, we may not see a tremendous difference in attitude, only fewer primary witnesses and survivors on hand.

Sandy Tankoos has allowed us to sit on the edges of our chairs as we parse out some of the major issues and questions of our time, and for that I am grateful.

Rabbi Josh Weinberg

Jewish Woman

I am Chosen
To be part of a stiffnecked people
A fossil in the archives of history

I am a child of Zion
Daughter of Sarah
Descendant of Queen Esther

I am a Woman
Through my veins flow
The Courage of Naomi
And the Wisdom of Deborah

I am a Remnant
of the Zealous Crusaders
the Spanish inquisitors
the Evil Hand of the Nazi exterminators

I am Eternal
A fragment of the Spirit of Masada
Joined in soul to my people Israel

Acknowledgments

I wrote the first few chapters of this book in 1994, shortly after I stepped down as President of my synagogue in Long Island. However, I was quite busy, dividing my time between my family, my business and my voluntary activities within the world of Jewish organizations, and I did not go back to writing until after I sold my business in 2006. I did finish writing the book at that time but did not do anything about it until a short while ago when family and friends encouraged me to try and have it published. I am most thankful to Wipf and Stock Publishers and their staff for giving me this opportunity.

I consider myself very fortunate because my family, my husband Ken, along with my three children, their spouses and my grandchildren are always supportive of every project I embark on, even when they think I'm misguided.

I do have a very special thank you to my daughter Jenine, who read the book and gave me much needed critical suggestions, to my son Robert, whose technical expertise, as always, proved to be invaluable in building a website for the book and directing my social media initiatives, and to my son Gary and my husband Ken for their optimism and reassurance that the book was worthy of publication. I am also, of course, very appreciative of those friends who read the book and gave me their opinions and suggestions, Joyce Rudnick, Vivian Abbott, and Jocie Wurzburg.

I also want to thank all of the rabbis, cantors, and lay volunteers I have worked with over the years whose wisdom and unselfishness continue to inspire me and who unquestionably influenced my writing.

Yiddish/Hebrew Words and Acronyms

Aliyah	Reading a portion from the Torah
Bar Mitzvah	A Jewish coming of age for boys at age 13
Bat Mitzvah	A Jewish coming of age for girls at age 13
B'not Mitzvah	Plural of Bat Mitzvah
Bube-meise	A grandmother's tale, fairytale
Gan Eden	The world to come
Goldene Medina	Golden Land
Goy	Person who is not Jewish
Halachah	Body of Jewish law
Hadassah	Organization of Jewish women working on behalf of Israel.
Kabbalistic	Mystic
Kaddish	Prayer recited for the dead
Kohane	Jewish priest
Mamzer	Bastard
Mazel tov	Good luck
Minyan	Quorum required for a prayer service
MOMA	Museum of Modern Art in New York City
Rebbetzen	Rabbi's wife
Reconstructionism	Liberal branch of Judaism

Sephardic	descendants of Jews who lived in Spain prior to the Spanish Inquisition
Shabbos	Sabbath
Shanda	A shame, scandal
Shekel	Currency of Israel
Shiva	Period of mourning
Shtetl	Small village in Eastern Europe
Shul	Synagogue
Siddur	Jewish daily prayer book
Tachlis	Purpose
Unveiling	Prayer service to mark the grave of the deceased with a headstone

Chapter One

D eborah was asleep, floating in and out of a fantasy world of anxiety-provoking dreams. As soon as she extricated herself from one troublesome nightmare, another would begin.

It was morning, time to get up, but once again she drifted off into an abyss, somewhere between slumber and awakening, a trance, where off in the distance she could see an image . . . a man approaching her bed . . . suddenly, a moment of recognition . . . it was Rabbi Levinson!

"Hello, Rabbi. What are you doing here? What are you doing in my dream?"

Rabbi Levinson was struggling to answer her. He seemed distraught. He was desperately trying to tell her something. He was motioning with his hands. Deborah could see his lips moving, she could feel his presence, but if he was speaking, she couldn't hear what he was saying and she couldn't understand what he wanted. The surrounding air felt heavy . . . stifling . . . suffocating. Her heart was pounding.

"Speak up, Rabbi," she said. "I can't hear you."

But Rabbi Levinson was himself gasping for breath and mouthing words that had no sound. Deborah reached out to touch him, but she could feel herself awakening while Rabbi Levinson still hovered above her bed, suspended in mid-air, larger than he ever was in real life.

"Rabbi?" Deborah called out, but there was no answer and without explanation the Rabbi disappeared. He was gone, fading away into the flowered wallpaper that covered the bedroom walls.

"What a dream," she thought, as she glanced over to the clock on the end table next to her bed. It was 8:45 in the morning. How had she allowed herself to sleep so late? Carl should have set the alarm for her. She jumped up and rushed toward the shower. She hated feeling rushed and being late for work. This was not a good omen for the rest of the day.

Deborah sat at the conference table in her office contemplating the papers in front of her. She had managed to get dressed and over to the office in record time, but although it was only 11:00 in the morning, she felt exhausted. She never set her alarm clock on days that she was not due in court; however, she had never before slept past 7:30. She took a moment to take several deep breaths, attempting to relieve the tension in her chest. Deborah had asked a law student interning with her to put together a rough draft of a brief, and last night she had stayed late at the office turning it into what at least one bankruptcy judge had dubbed "A Deborah Katzman Special."

Deborah Katzman, Esquire had worked long and hard for the respect she commanded among her peers. She had a thriving law practice and over time had become more and more selective about the cases she agreed to handle. "Lawyering" had not always been so favorable. Back in the sixties, female law school students were few and far between. Ten women had entered NYU Law School with her, but she was the only one among them to graduate. While in law school Deborah had been befriended early on by Susan King, a female student two classes ahead of her. She and Susan both possessed the inner strength and the ability to keep their eye on the target while moving full speed ahead. They also had in common that they were each more interested in their studies than they were in finding husbands—a fact that may have made their families unhappy, but did make graduation and passing the dreaded Bar exam more of a reality.

Susan went out into the real world after graduation, giving Deborah the advantage of being able to learn from her friend's experience. Since there were few private-sector jobs open to women at that point in time, Susan had accepted a position with the Manhattan D.A.'s office. She received little respect and was often the butt of office jokes. Her daily on-the-job experience quickly turned her youthful idealism into cynicism.

Deborah never forgot the phone conversation they had at the end of Susan's first week on the job, "Wait till you hear this one," she exclaimed, sounding close to hysteria, "my boss told me that he would never allow me to become a litigator because he's afraid I might get my period in the middle of a trial and 'crap everything up.'"

"So, what did you tell him?"

"I told him that I've had a hysterectomy and I don't get my period anymore."

"Good thinking!" Deborah laughed loudly. "So, did he buy it?"

"Who knows? The point is, we just always have to be the best there is. What these narrow-minded bastards want is for us to be polite and play the game their way . . . we're supposed to sit quietly in the back of the bus, and maybe, if we're lucky, the powers that be will recognize our ability and hand us a lollipop."

Deborah wasn't sure if Susan was right or wrong in her assessment, but Deborah Katzman (nee Benowitz) had no intention of taking a back seat to anyone. She didn't want to consider social service or public-sector law, which for the most part were the only fields open to women of her generation. As a Holocaust survivor she had seen enough physical suffering to last her a lifetime, and she knew she would never be able to survive a job that required her to deal with needy children on a daily basis.

What Deborah wanted was mental stimulation and to earn respect for her own competence. If no one would hire her, she would create her own law practice . . . maybe she could become so successful that even men would seek out her expertise.

Deborah rented a modest office and hung a shingle on her door. She began by handling bankruptcy cases at a price that attracted many buyers. There was no shortage of bankruptcies. Men running small businesses that were about to go under due to lack of funds were happy to accept the services of anyone who could help them, and Deborah soon became a familiar face in Bankruptcy Court. She knew she spent far more time on each case than any of her male counterparts might find necessary, but this was the seventies, and she had no choice. Her work product had to be better than perfect, it had to radiate brilliance.

Eventually judges began to commend her both publicly and privately for her professionalism, and now, all these years later, Deborah was sought after by those who wanted the best. She chose only those cases she found interesting, a "boutique practice," other lawyers would say, and that suited her just fine. She had earned it; it was hers, and she took great pleasure in contemplating her own success.

Deborah was deep in thought when she was abruptly interrupted by her secretary, Nancy, knocking on the door.

"Leon Feldman is on the phone. I told him you couldn't be disturbed, but he says it's urgent."

Deborah sighed, "Tell him I'll call him back as soon as I have time. I don't need the distraction of synagogue business right now."

Deborah well understood that she was being obsessive. The brief was basically finished, but she could afford to leave no sentence unanalyzed. These days women attorneys were all over the courts and she certainly had nothing left to prove, but old habits are hard to break and brilliance had become her standard.

"We're part of a dying breed," Susan had suggested recently. "Soon it will be just us and the dinosaurs."

Susan King had also managed to create a name for herself over the years. She had become a tough litigator after all, "Perpetual P.M.S." some of her opponents would complain, angry at her uncompromising demeanor or her ability to get the better of them. On those occasions she would call her good friend Deborah, and they would both laugh remembering what had happened her first week in the D.A.'s office. Eventually Susan left public service and joined a law firm that specialized in criminal law. And ten years ago, she too opened her own practice, taking two other women she worked with along with her. "I'm tired of having to cooperate with men who think they've won a victory by getting a rapist off with a suspended sentence," Susan proclaimed. "I want to pick and choose the cases my office handles."

Deborah and Susan had remained friends and colleagues over the years. They were bonded together in sisterhood from their shared experiences and had respect for each other professionally, but in their private lives they traveled in two different worlds. Back when they were in law school Deborah had assumed Susan was introverted and asexual. She, along with most of America, wasn't tuned in to alternate lifestyles. However, in recent years Susan had become very outspoken about gay and lesbian rights. She shared an apartment in Greenwich Village with a female elementary school teacher who Deborah had met at occasional Bar Association events. Deborah and Susan's conversations were limited to the subjects they shared in common. In other arenas they respected each other's privacy and lifestyle.

Chapter Two

November 16, 1992

N ancy opened the door once again. "Mr. Feldman is being very persistent. He says it is urgent and he has to speak to you."

Deborah moaned, but she was not surprised. Since becoming President of Beth Torah, she found that time had become an elusive element in her life. Leon Feldman was the Administrator of the synagogue. She picked up the phone on the desk next to her. "This had better be good, Leon," Deborah mumbled through her teeth, sounding as irritated as she felt at the moment.

"I hope you're sitting," he said.

"I'm fine with standing. Just tell me what you're calling about. I have a brief to finish."

Leon answered; his voice was devoid of all emotion, "The Rabbi has been shot. They took him away in an ambulance."

Deborah attempted to speak. She opened her mouth, but no words would come out. Suddenly she shrieked, "What did you say?" But she interrupted him before he could answer. "Who shot him?"

"I don't know. I heard a loud noise and I ran in. He was bleeding all over the floor. I called 911. The police came, an ambulance came, it was just crazy." Leon obviously had had some time to collect himself before calling her. He sounded very much in control of whatever it was that was going on.

"How badly is he hurt?"

"Oh, it's pretty bad. When I first got to him he was awake, but by the time the ambulance arrived he was unconscious. He didn't look too good to me, but what do I know?"

"What time did this happen?" she asked. Deborah was barely able to utter a sound, and to add to her overwhelming shock, as Leon spoke she remembered her dream of Rabbi Levinson suspended in the air over her bed. Suddenly she felt prickly goose bumps erupting all over her body.

"I know we were both here before 7:30. It must have been around 8:15 when the ambulance arrived."

"I'll call you back, I need a few minutes to collect myself." Deborah spoke slightly above a whisper, as though her vocal chords were paralyzed, but in her heart she knew—Rabbi Levinson was dead. And somehow, for some reason, he had chosen to make contact with her before he drifted off to . . .

She looked up and realized Nancy was staring at her. She had come running in upon hearing her scream.

"Are you all right?" Nancy asked, "You look pale."

"Someone has shot Rabbi Levinson." Deborah's mouth felt dry, and she began to tremble. "I think he's dead. Please, can you get me some water?"

"Of course." Nancy turned and walked briskly out the door.

Deborah fell into her chair. The brief staring up at her would have to be delivered as is. She had wanted to read it through one more time, but at this moment it no longer seemed important.

Chapter Three

April 2, 1992

"We really need you to run for President," insisted the three-person scout team from the synagogue that paid her a surprise visit one evening last spring. "It will put an end to all of the hysteria that's going on."

"That's absurd," she had replied.

"Not absurd at all," asserted Barry Weinstein, the Executive Vice President and heir apparent to the presidency of Beth Torah.

"I've only been a board member for one year. I don't even think I managed to get to half the meetings. I understand almost nothing about what's happening within the synagogue and everyone knows that. How can I be President?"

"For all of those reasons, you are perfect. Everyone loves you; no one will scream about synagogue politics, you haven't had time to develop adversaries. In fact, in all probability no one would even consider running against you. You're a shoe-in. The Rabbi will be thrilled to have you. The women will stop complaining. I'm telling you, it's the ideal solution," Barry said with assurance. "I'll be there helping you all the way, I promise." He sounded so sincere. Deborah knew he really believed every word he spoke.

"What do you think, Carl?" she had asked, turning to her husband, expecting him to be at least as unenthusiastic as she was about the idea.

"It's an honor and you'll probably enjoy it," he responded, beaming with pride on her behalf.

"But everything at the synagogue is in chaos right now. It just seems like there will be too much pressure on me."

Deborah had forgotten for the moment that Carl had always been too busy and uninterested to pay much attention to things that went on at synagogue. He went to pray on Rosh Hashanah, Yom Kippur, and on other infrequent occasions when she thought it important for him to attend.

"Well, both boys are grown and they've moved out of the house, so it seems to me this would give you something other than work to really be involved in."

"I'm not sure you understand how much time this is going to take," she answered.

"You know that ultimately this is your decision," Carl replied. "Do what you think is best."

"The point is," Barry interrupted, "that we believe you will be able to put an end to all of this hysteria that's going on."

"Yes, that's true," said Simmy Monash, in a heavy Mideastern accent. Simmy was from Iran and was the current President of Brotherhood. He tended to be overly dramatic about any situation that involved the synagogue and even more so if it involved the Rabbi. "And think of our poor Rabbi—he'll finally have some peace. I cry for him every night," his voice broke and he reached into his pocket for a crumpled handkerchief. "This is just for a short time. Maybe a year, that's all. That's enough. Then Barry can take over. We'll all help you." Simmy smiled and their eyes met.

"They're right, you know," spoke Rochelle Levy, the President of Sisterhood and the third member of the scout team. Rochelle and her husband Harry were a couple completely devoted to Beth Torah. They were among the elite group who were considered by everyone to be the backbone of the synagogue. "The women will be thrilled to have a female as President," Rochelle continued, "and the men think you're like one of them, so they'll be happy too. The Rabbi nearly jumped for joy when we ran your name by him last night. You've got to do it. Isn't that right, Harry?" she asked, turning to her husband who was sitting quietly in a corner, reading the newspaper.

"If Rochelle says so, it's got to be," Harry answered, smiling at his wife. "I learned a long time ago, Rochelle is always right."

1968

Beth Torah was a Conservative Synagogue located on the *exclusive* North Shore of Long Island. It was housed in a former mansion, a magnificent Tudor-type building set back off what was once a small country road, on ten carefully landscaped acres. Its membership consisted mostly of middle-to-upper-income families, which was reflective of the surrounding neighborhood. Rabbi Levinson loved the congregation and during those early years the congregation had been as unanimous as any synagogue could be in its love for him.

Before Rabbi Levinson had joined them, Beth Torah had simply been called "The Synagogue in the Woods," which, after all, described it quite explicitly. And since all of the members were certain that theirs was the best synagogue that could be found anywhere, they had started referring to it merely as "*The* Synagogue," dropping "in the Woods" from the title completely, and always putting an emphasis on "The," which gave the impression that they were the "only" synagogue in town, though this was certainly not the case.

Soon after Rabbi Levinson accepted their pulpit he chided them for appearing to be "too elitist," and strongly suggested they change the name to be more in keeping with Jewish values. Since many members had opinions that had to be considered, it took more than six months for the congregation to make the decision to actually go ahead and change the name, and another year to come to an agreement on just what that new name should be, but eventually "*The* Synagogue" became "Synagogue Beth Torah," a name that would give their sacred Torahs the prominence they deserved. Nevertheless, many members still referred to it as "*The* Synagogue," because to those who loved its hallowed walls, that is exactly what it was.

Like all synagogues, the board members of Beth Torah always had many issues to consider and debate, but theirs had been a congenial group. They were dedicated to having the best religious school, the best adult-ed programming, and the most active sisterhood and brotherhood of any synagogue in the area.

As the years went by Beth Torah developed a wonderful reputation for being a sharing-and-caring congregation, and its membership grew and grew and grew. Before long, they were the largest synagogue on the north shore of Long Island, with a Rabbi whose wonderful reputation was the envy of his colleagues both near and far.

Deborah had gone to visit three synagogues before deciding which one her family would join. Carl's family had never been active in any synagogue. "Whatever you think," he had told her. "You know more about this than I do. Just pick one."

Rabbi Levinson had made the decision easy. He was so kind and gentle that once meeting him there was no choice. Since he had already been there for many years by the time Deborah and Carl Katzman and family joined, Deborah believed there wasn't much chance of his leaving. Her own father had not survived the Nazi death camp at Treblinka and she had almost no memory of him, but Deborah tended to compare all important men in her life to a God-like image of the father she never knew, and though Rabbi Levinson was close to her own age, he was the intellectual yet benevolent and tender man she inevitably sought out.

April 2, 1992

"I need some time to think about it," Deborah Katzman had told the scout team after being offered the presidency of Beth Torah. "I'll let you know by the weekend."

"What do you think, Barry?" Simmy asked upon leaving the Katzman home.

"What do I think? I think flattery is everything. She's in."

"I hope you're right. I can't stand much more of this," sighed Rochelle. "I cry about it constantly. All of the younger women in Sisterhood are talking about quitting and forming a new Reform synagogue. Even Harry can't believe what's going on here; isn't that right, Harry?"

Harry and Rochelle were an unusually devoted couple. Harry was ten years older than Rochelle and he often referred to her as his "child bride." They could be seen holding hands or sharing many private moments together, even at large gatherings of people. Everyone at Beth Torah admired their loving relationship. Harry had a way of gazing at Rochelle with such love that all the Sisterhood women could tell at a glance what a wonderful husband he was. Harry would do anything for Rochelle, and often did.

"If Rochelle says so, how could it be anything else?" Harry replied.

"I agree with Barry," said Simmy with conviction. "For a woman to be offered such a thing, she would be crazy to say no." Simmy smiled and Rochelle cringed.

"She is a lawyer, you know," Rochelle mumbled in a low voice. Oh, she understood what he meant; becoming the first woman President of "*The* Synagogue" would certainly be an honor for Deborah Katzman, or any other woman, but although Rochelle Levy had belonged to Beth Torah for more than twenty years and wasn't one of these young demanding women causing them so much trouble, she did have a mind of her own, and Rochelle decided she certainly could do without Simmy's old-world machismo.

Simmy laughed and put his arm around her shoulder. "Come, come now, since when did you become a 'libber?'"

Rochelle clenched her teeth tightly together, but she said nothing. There already was enough dissension within their sacred walls to form four or five synagogues. She couldn't be fighting with her friends. She would work out her feelings by discussing it with Harry as soon as they got home.

It was hard to figure out just when things began to go wrong at Beth Torah. Deborah had thought about that often over the last few months. If she could pinpoint a moment in time when it all started to unravel, perhaps she could figure out how to put it back together.

"You just have to be a caretaker for a short while," Barry had insisted, "just until things become normal again. Then, we will take it from there. We need someone like you as a transition person, someone to bring sanity into all of this madness."

She knew that Barry never had any intention of deceiving her, but what she had come to realize and he just didn't understand was things could never go back to what he and his friends considered to be "normal," because "normal" had changed. The unfolding events had taught her that Barry Weinstein, for all his good intentions, was part of the problem, a leader who insisted upon marking time in place, remaining an observer as the world around them marched forward.

Chapter Four

R abbi Saul Levinson graduated from Yeshiva University in 1958. He
was a deeply religious man who had grown up in a traditional Orthodox family. His grandfather was the Orthodox Rabbi of their neighborhood *shul*. His father was a doctor who worked as a general practitioner in
Flatbush, Brooklyn, where he had lived with his wife since the day he got
married. His family was financially very comfortable. Saul lived with his
parents in a two-family house. There was one apartment on the ground
level and another one flight up. Dr. Levinson's office was located on the
ground floor; the family lived in the apartment above the office.

Dr. Levinson was well respected within their community; everyone
who used his services spoke of him with deep reverence. He was Orthodox
by tradition rather than by temperament. He tried to make as much time
for his wife, his son, and his parents as he could, but his medical practice
kept him so busy that if his office weren't located in the house, Saul probably would hardly have seen them at all. For Dr. Levinson, his patients were
his passion and he had little time for anything other than the rudiments of
a kosher lifestyle and, when his practice allowed it, an occasional *minyan*,
in deference to his father, the Rabbi.

Saul's mother and father were extraordinarily compatible. His mother
was thrilled to be married to a doctor. She would introduce herself as
"Sonia Levinson, Dr. Levinson's wife," as if that fact was her most defining
characteristic. Sonia became a Life Member of Hadassah. She was active
within her local chapter, and rose quickly within its ranks. She spent her
time working hard for Jewish Federation and Israel, knowing her status

in the community as the wife of Dr. Levinson was very helpful in all she accomplished on their behalf. A harder worker than Sonia Levinson was impossible to find.

Saul's grandparents rented a small apartment in the house next door. Saul especially loved to be with his grandfather and accompanied him to *shul* almost every day. Grandpa Levinson's religious fervor was passionate and inspiring. The old man told him wonderful stories of what life had been like growing up as a child in Romania before Hitler. In the old country Grandpa Levinson was an important man, he was "a something"; people respected him and his learning. And while there were still a scant group of men who had not forgotten, and occasionally there would even be some-one who traveled a great distance to have Grandpa bless him or help him resolve a complicated personal problem, he never achieved the same status he had enjoyed in the "Old Country."

"Always it's better to be a big fish in a small pond," Grandpa would tell him. "Here in America, suddenly I was a nothing. Too many Rabbis, too few observant Jews. But in the old country," he would say, with his eyes sparkling, "there people knew who I was! There I was a something! We could have gone to Palestine, but the British, those *mamzers,* wouldn't let us in. There I would have been with our own people. I could be studying all the time. In Palestine I wouldn't be struggling to get a *minyan* every night. Al-ways remember, Saulie, for a Jew there is no place but to be with other Jews. We have to be with our own kind, to stay together and try to rebuild some of what that maniac Hitler took away from us. Those of us who understand, it's our obligation, we have to teach the others."

Grandma Levinson spent most of her time in the kitchen. She did all the cooking for both families and the aromas coming from that apartment gave Saul a feeling of comfort that as an adult he was never able to duplicate.

Saul could remember being sick and Grandma arriving with a home-made ointment she rubbed all over his chest. It smelled awful, but felt won-derful. She would sit next to him and rub it in slowly and gently. By the time she was finished Saul would feel almost healed. Grandma always had strange kinds of herbs she would mix together over the stove with different oils or water. She would take the subway to someplace called "The East Side" to buy them. The strength of the mixture depended on the severity of the illness. His father and grandmother had an ongoing battle that would begin anew each time grandma would insist upon treating a cold with some strange-tasting tea, or use a mushy paste to clear up a bruise.

"Mamma, I have real medicine to give him, he doesn't need these *buba-meisas*," Saul's father would say.

And Grandma would answer, "What's the matter, Mr. Big Shot Doctor? You think my medicine isn't real? This medicine has kept our people alive for generations. It's a proven product, and I give it with love."

No matter what his mother and father thought, Saul always knew that Grandma's medicines were the best. After each one of Grandma's treatments, Grandpa would come to sit by his bed and hold his hand; they would listen to the radio or play cards, if he felt well enough. Grandpa was his best friend. Saul lived with his parents, but his soul belonged to Grandma and Grandpa, and until he met Esther, they were the people who had the strongest influence on his life.

While an undergraduate student at Yeshiva University Saul met and fell in love with Esther Klein, a student at Barnard College. Esther came from a modern, secular, Jewish family. Her parents were socialists who believed their daughter should be as well educated as their son. Saul wanted to be a Rabbi like his grandfather, but Esther let him know early on that his grandparents' Orthodox lifestyle was too oppressive for her. She loved him and was willing to make certain compromises, but if orthodoxy was what he expected of a wife, they would have to part ways.

Saul was sympathetic to her feelings and certainly agreed that a husband and wife should be able to sit together during prayer services and live a more global existence than his grandparents. So, feeling that both rabbinical school and Esther were each too important to abandon, he and Esther determined together that it would be best for him to attend Jewish Theological Seminary, where he would study to become a Conservative Rabbi. They were married in August, shortly before the beginning of the school year.

JTS was Rabbi Levinson's introduction to the Conservative Movement. If he was going to be a Rabbi, Esther wanted him to concentrate on his studies and become the most respected and learned Rabbi in his class. Grandpa assured him his bride was right and this was the most important thing he could do for himself. Esther insisted he finish all his education before going out to work in the "real world." She was a social worker and was able to support them both on her income, albeit not in great luxury, but it was certainly enough to accommodate their modest needs.

Saul Levinson dutifully became a very outstanding student. There were many bonuses about becoming a Conservative Rabbi as opposed to an

Orthodox Rabbi; most important in those early years was that as a young Orthodox couple, Esther and Saul Levinson would have been expected to have children immediately, but as a young Conservative couple, waiting a few years to start a family would not be unusual. They agreed it would be best to put off having a baby until Saul was working in a congregation of his own. The five years of rabbinical school were happy ones, and the time went by very quickly.

While in his last year at JTS, Saul and Esther discussed the type of congregation Saul should look for. He could go into a large congregation as an Assistant Rabbi and have an opportunity to learn by observing and training with a Master, or he could elect to go to a pulpit of his own in a smaller community where he would have more responsibility and, as he and Esther saw it, greater opportunity to grow as a Rabbi by having to do it all himself.

"Two things you should look for," Grandpa advised him. "Go where you'll be respected and where you can continue to study but go where you can make a difference. Spend a few weekends in the community before tying yourself down to a contract. Count how many Jewish people there are. You don't want to be isolated . . . for a Jew to be isolated is the worst thing."

However, despite Grandpa's advice, he and Esther had lived in or near New York City all of their lives and the quality of life in small-town America was very appealing to both of them. Esther wanted to work in a place where she could truly reach out to help those in need, rather than continue to struggle with the big-city bureaucracy that exacerbated the misfortunes of the persecuted and heightened their frustrations. Saul envisioned a small-town synagogue as being the life of the Jewish community, a place where people would come to expand their minds and delve deep into their souls. He could be the big fish in the little pond Grandpa had always talked about.

Rabbi Levinson was interviewed for a 200-family-member pulpit in Green County, New York, a short two-and-a-half-hour drive from Manhattan. Coincidentally, at the same time, a nearby hospital was searching for a social worker to head up an alcohol and drug abuse program. Esther and Saul did not investigate the community they would be living in as Saul was certain that God's hand was truly visible in leading them to this place. They prepared to move, impatient to validate their dreams, knowing it was they themselves, not other people, who would create their own Jewish experience. Soon it would be time to start their own family.

Rabbi and Esther Levinson moved into a small, synagogue-owned house in Green County, New York. They arrived full of enthusiasm, but reality was not long in coming. Esther observed almost immediately that the local environment was hostile to both herself and to the population of people she was working with. She was totally unable to achieve any measure of success or satisfaction with her job. There appeared to be a general belief within the surrounding community that those who really wanted to could pull themselves up by their own bootstraps and that her salary was an unnecessary frill to burden the tax rolls.

"Even massive bureaucracy is more excusable than total intolerance of these poor unfortunate souls," she would cry to Saul. "I don't seem to be able to do anything to help."

Even worse, Rabbi Levinson soon learned that the hub of the Jewish population in Green County, New York was the Jewish golf club. Each Saturday the parking lot at the club was filled to capacity, while unless there was a Bar Mitzvah, he couldn't even scrape a *minyan* together for the morning prayers.

"Maybe you should join the golf club, Saul," Esther suggested naively. "If you get to know the members of the club then maybe they'll start coming to synagogue."

"Has anyone invited me to become a guest of the club? Do you think we can afford to join on a Rabbi's salary?"

"Well, maybe you could go over and inquire, and if they see you're interested perhaps they'll extend an invitation."

Saul didn't have to think very long before answering, "No, I don't think so. I don't like the image of a Rabbi on the take. If they wanted me as a member, they could invite me without my asking. And even then I'm not so sure Grandpa would think that was ethical."

There were no more than a handful of members supporting the synagogue; the others were either unwilling or unable. Educational programming was almost nonexistent and there was no one for Saul to study with. Also, to their great surprise, Esther and Saul discovered the cost of living was actually much higher than it had been in New York City. There were no discount clothing stores nearby. They had to drive more than forty-five minutes to buy kosher meat, and it cost almost double the inflated prices they had become accustomed to paying in Manhattan. The Rabbi's salary was barely enough for them to live on, even with the house the congregation provided to them. They may have been able to live rent free, but the winters were cold and the house was not well insulated. There were months when the price of heat and electric was so exorbitant that they had to borrow money from their parents to make the payments. For the first time in their lives they felt poor, and worst of all, Esther seemed unable to conceive. She became despondent and spent many weekends lying in bed, not choosing even to talk to Saul.

"Come back home," Dr. Levinson told his son. "New York City is where Jews belong, and here there are doctors who can help Esther."

Rabbi Levinson assured his wife that theirs was just a temporary situation. They had not chosen wisely the first time, but they were still young enough to learn from the experience and move on. Someone with his scholastic record and some work history would have no difficulty doing better. They just had to wait it out. Time was on their side. They understood clearly where they had gone wrong. What they needed was a larger, more affluent, Jewish community. Someplace where a Rabbi was treated with respect and given a salary commensurate with his education. And his father was right, it was important to be near doctors who would help Esther conceive the baby they both desperately yearned for. They would go back to the New York City area, only this time they would seek out a suburb that would be compatible with their own ideals.

Although it was still more than a year before he could give notice that he would leave at the end of his contract, preparing for the next job helped make each day a bit more tolerable.

Saul and Esther discussed the skills Saul would have to cultivate in order to secure a job in a more sophisticated Jewish community, and they set about working toward that goal. He studied sermonizing with the same intensity as an actor studying for the stage. Esther was his audience, and she was not easy to please.

"Let your voice break, when you mention Israel," she would tell him. "Be passionate. Speak louder. You have to get their attention."

And he listened and did as she said.

Clearly, too, if Saul wanted to get a position in a prestigious congregation, it would help if he could distinguish himself as a Rabbi in some fashion. Esther found the perfect opportunity. The year was 1968 and a group of confused, disaffected flower children somehow found their way into the local landscape. Anywhere from eleven to sixteen young men and women lived together in a dilapidated house they rented just outside of Hudson, New York. Several of them worked as orderlies and kitchen help at the hospital. They were harmless enough, but given their slovenly appearance and the local paranoia, the police had picked them up for loitering on a number of occasions while they were walking through town. They bemoaned their fate to Esther at the hospital, and she was incensed over the callousness of the police and the local newspaper hype that seemed to follow their every move. This was a real human rights issue, one that a Rabbi should rightfully get himself involved with.

Esther and Saul had discussed the problem and what he might do about it. One *Shabbos* morning, on their way home from *shul*, they noticed a crowd gathered in front of the supermarket. Strolling over, they found two policemen addressing a young man with a sparse beard and long, straggly brown hair. His stained jeans had holes in the middle of both knees. With him was an equally young, painfully thin girl with freckles and auburn hair that hung down to her waist. She was dressed in tight-fitting, dark blue corduroy pants. Both were wearing red T-shirts with a large white dove painted across their chests.

"I've told you before, you're not allowed to sit here and loiter," announced a short, stout policeman in a much louder voice than anyone would think necessary.

"We're not doing nothing," answered the male loiterer.

"Well, you can't do it here," the officer bellowed, pulling a set of handcuffs out of his pocket.

"Do something, Saul," Esther screamed. "I can't stand this."

Saul approached the second officer, a thin, balding man who had prominent red veins all around his nose. "Excuse me, Officer, I'm Rabbi Levinson."

"We're busy right now, Rabbi."

"So I see. Are you arresting these young people?"

"Yes, we are. Get out of our way, please."

"Why are you arresting them?"

"What do you care for?"

"I do care."

"You know these bums, Rabbi?"

"No, I don't."

"So, what's your problem?"

"I want to know why they're under arrest."

"For loitering. They're loitering."

"These cops are pigs, Rabbi, we're not doing nothing," cried the freckle-faced girl. "I'm Jewish, Rabbi. Don't let them take me."

"I believe these young people's civil rights are being violated," Saul calmly continued. "Since when is it a crime to be standing in a shopping mall?"

"Go home, Rabbi," shouted someone from the crowd. "We don't want these damn hippies around here."

"Why don't you go home?" screamed Esther.

"Listen to me, all of you," proclaimed Rabbi Levinson to the crowd of people that was growing larger and louder by the minute. "If you don't see to it that these young people's civil rights are protected today, the police can come and trample over your civil rights tomorrow."

"Get out of the way, Rabbi," shouted the stout policeman, "You're interfering with an arrest."

"With the help of God I certainly am," Saul retorted.

"Get out of the way or we're going to toss you into the car along with them, Rabbi."

"No, you can't," Saul responded. "As an observant Jew, I am not permitted to ride in an automobile on the Sabbath."

"No more talk, just move," the stout policeman pushed Saul over to the side.

"How dare you strike a Rabbi," shrieked Esther. "He's a man of God. You have no respect."

"Take them both in," the officer with the red nose hollered out to his buddy.

"I told you, I can't ride in a car on *Shabbos*," Rabbi Levinson declared again.

"You should have thought of that before you and your old lady put your two cents in, Rabbi," shouted the red nose. "Both of you get into the car," he said, pushing Esther by the elbow.

"Saul, I'm so proud of you," Esther whispered, smugly grabbing hold of his hand.

The headlines in the New York City newspapers read: "Rabbi Arrested on Sabbath Demanding Civil Rights for Hippies."

"They made you get into the car on *Shabbos*?" Grandpa was so shocked he could barely speak. "How could this happen in America?!"

"Come home," demanded Dr. Levinson. "It's enough already!"

"The Anti-Defamation League will be there to interview you tomorrow. I arranged it," proclaimed the Rabbi's mother.

Esther's parents were beaming with pride to think their daughter would go to jail just to protect the civil rights of other human beings, no matter what their race or religion was.

They had become famous and respected not only in the Jewish community, but by the entire City of New York. The time had come at last to look for a new job.

"Why is the present Rabbi leaving?" Saul inquired of the placement director at the Jewish Theological Institute.

"His contract is not being renewed. This is an intellectual, affluent congregation. They want someone who knows how to deliver a sermon, who's not afraid to take on important issues. This is an active community."

Saul felt the adrenaline rush to his head.

"This is ours," Esther assured him. "This is the one we've been preparing for these past two years."

It took only two interviews and three telephone conversations until Esther and Rabbi Saul Levinson were able to pack and move happily to the north shore of Long Island.

Chapter Five

August 1968

The local newspaper headlines read: "Synagogue Welcomes Civil Rights Rabbi and His Wife to the North Shore."

Synagogue life on the north shore was better than either Saul or Esther could ever have imagined. Rabbi Levinson arrived as a celebrity. People came from near and far to listen to him speak out on important issues, and he did not disappoint them.

"That man could recite the phone book, and everyone would listen," his congregants would say.

But Saul didn't recite the phone book; he was passionate about human rights, the evils of the Vietnam War, and as time went by, most especially about Israel. Year after year, Temple Beth Torah consistently ran the most successful UJA breakfasts and Israel Bond functions in the state. When Rabbi Levinson asked, people did not refuse. A portion of all the money raised on behalf of the synagogue had to be syphoned off for Israel—on this, there was no compromise for Rabbi Levinson. Saul's mother's face beamed with pride. She was sure it was her influence that made her son such a strong Zionist.

At home with Esther, Saul proclaimed, "All these years later, and everything my grandfather taught me is still true. If I had listened to him to begin with, we would have made fewer mistakes."

Esther heard him, but said nothing.

1970

Synagogue life may have proved to be wonderful, but for Esther the world was still bleak. She had gone to three doctors within two years of moving to Long Island, but none of them were able to help her conceive.

"Nothing is wrong, Mrs. Levinson," they each told her. "Go on a vacation and relax, that's the best thing you can do for yourself."

Esther was taking her temperature each morning and charting it carefully on graph paper. Sex had become a chore that she and Saul had to perform whenever the numbers were right.

"We're like bookies always checking these damn numbers," she would sigh, but unfortunately, even when the numbers were right, something was still wrong and nothing happened.

On a rare Sunday visit to her in-laws, Esther was bemoaning her fate.

"Don't think I don't understand, darling," her mother-in-law responded sympathetically. "It took me several years to conceive Saul, and even though I always tried to have another baby, I never could, and no one ever knew why. You know, Dr. Levinson and I have never done anything to prevent another pregnancy. It simply never happened."

"I didn't know that. I assumed you didn't want any more children," Esther answered, not attempting to hide her amazement.

"Of course not. I wanted a daughter too. Doesn't every woman want a daughter? I mean, my Saul is wonderful, and I love him, but I always dreamed of having a daughter."

Esther wanted to say something comforting like, "Well, you now have me," but they both knew better. She and her mother-in-law had come to an early truce. Their love for Saul allowed them to tolerate each other, but the extraordinary concern that Esther displayed for people she characterized as poor and oppressed, many of whom weren't even Jewish, seemed excessive to her mother-in-law, while Esther considered Sonia Levinson to be a pitiful featherhead whose main goal in life was to achieve constant recognition for herself based upon the accomplishments of her family.

For several days Esther dwelled on this new information Sonia had given her, fascinated by the fact that she and her mother-in-law finally had something in common.

"Of course, she still has Saul," Esther commented when reiterating the story to her own mother. "I have nothing."

Esther began to wonder, Was it possible that both the Great Dr. Levinson and his son, the Rabbi, had some sort of inherited genetic problem? She decided to speak to her gynecologist about it at the next visit. She was due to bring in her temperature chart on Monday.

Dr. Lieb, the gynecologist that Esther was currently using, was Chief of Gynecology at Mt. Sinai Hospital in Manhattan. He listened attentively while Esther related her new information.

"It's been my experience that it's usually the woman who has the problem, but certainly, we should check out your husband too, just to know that we have eliminated that as a source of your infertility."

Saul was shocked at the suggestion that he might be the cause of Esther's inability to conceive a baby. Obviously, if his mother had conceived even once, his father had not had a real problem. Nevertheless, just to be fair, he would allow his sperm to be tested.

Several days later Esther arrived back at Dr. Lieb's office carrying a sterilized bottle filled with Saul's sperm to be examined under the microscope.

"Well, this is interesting," Dr. Lieb muttered, "the sperm count here is not too good. Not impossible, mind you, but not too good; somewhat unlikely, I'm sorry to say."

Unlike her mother-in-law, Esther Levinson never did conceive even one baby.

"We could adopt," she would cry to Saul when they were lying in bed at night.

"I don't want someone else's baby, and how could we make sure the baby was really Jewish?"

"Once we adopt a baby it doesn't belong to someone else, it belongs to us, and if there's any doubt about religion, the baby can be converted. Please, Saul," she would beg.

"No. We'll keep trying. It's not impossible, the doctor said so. After all, if my father did have the same problem, my very existence is proof that our turn will come. Look how old Sarah was when she gave birth to Isaac."

"Oh, God. Get real, Saul! Now I have to listen to lectures from Scripture. Who do you think I am, one of your adoring congregants? Don't tell me you actually believe that a ninety-year-old woman gave birth to a baby."

"Well, age may have been arrived at a little differently, but one thing we know for sure, Sarah was well beyond the age when a woman would normally be expected to have a baby."

Esther found his attitude infuriating. What was worse, she couldn't bear to be surrounded by all of the mothers in the neighborhood. Sisterhood luncheons had become excruciatingly painful events she chose not to attend. All anyone ever spoke about was what was going on at the PTA or which store was having a sale on children's clothing. Over Saul's objections, Esther went back to work as a social worker.

"We're a team," he told her. "The Rabbi and Rebitzen working together to build a congregation.

"We're no team. We can't even make a baby together. This is your life not mine, and I'm not your mother. If I can't raise my own child like any other wife walking around in this community, I at least have to spend my time doing something that's important to me."

Esther went to work for Jewish Foster Care Service and spent most of her days trying to find homes for unwanted children.

Saul was uncomfortable attending Sisterhood luncheons without Esther being there. Many of the women would ask where she was and everyone would send their regards along with their hope that she might join them next time. He knew this turn of events was not being well-received by the Sisterhood leadership, but he didn't want his personal life to be a matter of discussion within the synagogue, so he chose not to give any explanation as to where Esther was. Saul was sitting in his office early one afternoon, contemplating an upcoming donor luncheon for Hadassah being hosted by the Sisterhood on the following day. He understood that the women, once again, would be puzzled at why he was attending alone. He decided to discuss the problem with his grandfather, and he dialed his number, but as fate would have it, Saul's mother was visiting with Grandpa and it was she who answered the phone.

"Hello, Mom. How are you doing?" he asked, suddenly realizing that a solution was within reach.

"I'm fine. Everyone is fine. I suppose you want to speak to Grandpa?"

"Actually, it's you I want to speak to," he answered.

"Is something wrong?"

"No, I just wondered if you would like to attend a luncheon with me tomorrow?"

"You'd like me to come?"

"Yes. It's an Hadassah donor luncheon. It would be very nice to have you with me. With Esther working I've been going alone and I think I'd feel better having some company, And I'm sure you'd enjoy it. You've always been active in Hadassah."

"What mother doesn't enjoy spending time with her son? Tell me when and you can be sure I'll be there."

Sonia Levinson quickly became a familiar figure at Beth Torah. She attended all Sisterhood functions and other events that required the Rabbi's presence. She sat at his side, glowing with pride whenever he got up to speak. With the help of a plastic surgeon and a personal trainer she maintained a stylish, youthful demeanor that brought her the admiration of all the women in the congregation. She played the role of "the Rebitzen" of Beth Torah with the same love and devotion she had given to all the other organizations she had worked for over the years, but this was even better, for here at Beth Torah all of her good deeds, everything she did, reflected well on her son. The women so enjoyed having Sonia with them, they barely remembered to ask about Esther.

1980

As time went by Rabbi Levinson spent more and more time with the children of his congregation. Young people flocked around him as though he were the Pied Piper.

"They are our future," he would tell anyone who asked, "This is the most important thing I do."

"Can you imagine," the congregants would weep, "that a man with such a love for our children could be married to a woman who doesn't want children!"

"She's so busy saving the world, she has no time to build a family."

"Poor Rabbi Levinson! Why he doesn't leave her, I'll never be able to figure out. I tell you he's a Jewish Saint."

The children of Beth Torah formed the largest Zionist Youth Group on Long Island. Saul prided himself on the numbers of young people each year who, under his influence, made "*Aliyah*" and moved to Israel. If some of their parents found separation from their children upsetting, it took only one conversation with their Rabbi for them to realize that these exceptional children were off on a greater mission than their parents could ever hope to achieve.

"A life line for the future of our people," the Rabbi would explain. "Our very essence is tied up in them. You should be proud that you raised such a child."

Chapter Six

"Mr. Feldman is on the phone again," said Nancy, laying the glass of water Deborah had requested on the table in front of her.

Deborah lifted the phone to her ear. "Hello, Leon," she mumbled.

"He's dead. I just got a call from the police. There's some detective on his way over to see you." Leon went on, "I didn't know where else to send him. Can you beat that?"

"The Rabbi's dead," she said out loud, not being able to erase from her mind the image of Rabbi Levinson as he had appeared before her earlier that morning, still finding it impossible to absorb all that had happened.

"Dead," Leon answered without any elaboration.

"Thank you for letting me know," she answered, realizing full well that due to the Rabbi's personal visit to her bedroom, she had been the first to know of his passing. "I'll be in touch later. I don't know what I'm doing, I need time to think."

"Sure, see you later," Leon replied.

Deborah placed the telephone back into its cradle and sat horrified in her chair.

"Murder!" she exclaimed in disbelief.

Who could have done such a thing, and was there something she could have done to prevent it? And if there was, did that make her guilty in some circuitous fashion for what occurred?

Deborah struggled to remember her dream. Why had Rabbi Levinson come to visit her? She shuddered and goose bumps appeared on her arms.

"Oh, my God," she said out loud, "I can't believe this is happening. Rabbi what were you trying to tell me?"

The buzzer on her intercom sounded.

"There's a Detective Brody here to see you," the receptionist announced.

"They sure didn't waste any time," she mumbled to herself. Deborah took a deep breath, "Okay, send him in."

Detective Brody had a pleasant, kind face and a mild manner; he was medium height, and while he wasn't heavy, his stomach protruded out and folded over his belt. He had a full head of wavy, graying hair.

"I'm sorry to intrude on you in the middle of your business day, Ms. Katzman, but I've been told you are the President of Beth Torah, and I assume you already know what has happened?"

His voice was calm and compassionate, not like somebody who did this thousands of times each year, as Deborah was sure he did.

"Yes, and I'm still in shock, and I'm trembling. I probably should go home, but I'm just too upset. I'm not sure what I should be doing. I've only been president a few months."

Deborah suddenly jumped up.

"Oh," she said out loud, "I should have called his wife. Poor Esther." Deborah was rambling.

"Well, of course, that's very understandable. Even though murder has become more commonplace, shooting a Rabbi? That's still not something that happens every day. That's unusual even where I come from."

With that, Deborah could no longer keep her composure, she began to cry uncontrollably and Detective Brody began to fidget uncomfortably in his seat.

"I'm sorry," she said, "please just give me a moment and I'll be okay. It's just that I'm still trying to absorb everything that's happened."

"Of course," he answered in that same soothing voice. "You take your time. Or if you prefer, perhaps I can speak to you later on in the day."

"No, no, I'll be fine. Just let me catch my breath, please."

At that moment her secretary buzzed her on the intercom. "Carl is on the phone," she announced, "and *Newsday* is here to speak to you."

"Forgive me for one minute, Detective Brody. I want to tell my husband what's happened," she said, swallowing hard and trying to collect herself.

"Of course. Would you like me to step out of the room?"

She hesitated before replying, "No, I don't see why that would be necessary."

Deborah picked up the phone. "Oh, Carl, something terrible has—"
But before she could finish her sentence, Carl interrupted.

"I know, I was in the hospital when they brought him in. In fact, I was one of the doctors who worked on him. He was still alive, although barely, when the ambulance arrived at the hospital, and we were trying to resuscitate him. I wanted to call you right away. I'm sorry I didn't, but Leon had called Esther and she was here at the hospital and falling apart. I just had to stay with her for a while. I didn't want to leave her alone. Are you okay?"

"You were the doctor who treated him," she exclaimed, "Oh, God, of course you would have been at the hospital. I can't imagine how that never occurred to me," Deborah responded.

"I tried to save him, I really did. There were four of us working on him, but he never had a chance, the bullet penetrated his heart and lungs, there was just too much damage and he lost a lot of blood. This one really hurts. I worked on him until the very end."

"Oh, of course. I can't bear just hearing about it, but having to actually treat him, trying to save him, I can't imagine it." Deborah was no longer crying, but her heart felt heavy, like a lead weight sitting in the middle of her chest, and it was aching.

"Just tell me quickly, before you hang up, how is Esther doing? It was wonderful of you to stay with her. As usual, you did good."

"She was as you would expect her to be. She was very hyper, crying one minute, jumping around the room the next, but she's a strong woman, and she'll manage I'm sure. Do you have to get to the synagogue or what?" he asked.

"Maybe later. There's a detective here to speak to me. And a reporter from *Newsday* is waiting outside. I'll call you back after things settle down," she said, smiling faintly at Detective Brody.

"I've got a room full of patients, let me call you when I'm finished here and I'll meet you. I'll see if I can get someone to cover for me tonight. It's going to be hard to get through this day."

Although he couldn't see her, Deborah nodded in agreement. "As soon as you are done I want to go over to see Esther. I don't think I can face her alone. Thank God that at least she had you with her when all of this happened. I'll wait for your call."

Detective Brody sat patiently, until she hung up the phone.

"I was not aware, Mrs. Katzman, that you didn't know that your husband was one of the physicians who treated Rabbi Levinson at the hospital."

"How could I know? I've been here all morning. Didn't this just happen?" Deborah was still trying to sort things out.

"Well, the Rabbi apparently arrived at the synagogue early this morning. He accidently set off the burglar alarm coming in, so we know that he arrived just before 7:15 a.m. The administrator, Mr. Feldman, arrived, according to what he told me, unusually early, just before 7:30. He spoke to the Rabbi and everything was fine at that point."

Deborah was waiting for him to finish the saga, but the detective was looking at her, no longer speaking, waiting for some response. "Then when did he get shot?" she asked.

Detective Brody continued, "Well, according to Mr. Feldman, he heard some shots at about a quarter to 8:00, and at that point he rushed down the steps and found Rabbi Levinson slumped over, still alive."

"How did they shoot him? I mean, what did they use?"

"Are you a criminal attorney, Mrs. Katzman."

"No," she responded, consciously deciding not to say anything else about her law practice at this point.

"I see. Well, ma'am, he was shot with a common pistol, a Colt 45, the kind some people like to keep in their homes. The gun was there on the floor at his side. We'll have to search our records, just on the chance that it was actually registered to someone. From where the gun dropped there's an outside chance that it was suicide, but this doesn't seem like a suicide to me."

"I just can't understand how somebody could get past Leon, into the Rabbi's office and shoot him so early in the morning."

"Actually, the Rabbi was not in his office, he was in the library, apparently reading a book."

Deborah had just assumed the Rabbi had been shot in his office, but the library . . .

"Well, that changes things a little bit," she said, obviously startled.

"Please enlighten me. How does that change things?" Detective Brody began fumbling in his pocket for a small pad he carried around to write notes on. "I think I need larger pockets," he quipped.

Deborah smiled. "Well, you see," she continued, "The library is in the basement of the synagogue and there's a door leading outside to the side of the building which isn't really visible from the street nor from any other part of the synagogue. There's not even a window over there. I couldn't figure out how someone could get past the front office with Leon there, but now I understand."

"And who is Leon?" Detective Brody was writing furiously in his book.

"Leon Feldman is the administrator. I thought you mentioned him before."

"I'm sorry, I did meet him, I just didn't remember his first name." Detective Brody eyes were focused on her.

"Mrs. Katzman, can you think of any enemies of the Rabbi, people who might want to see him dead?"

Deborah was weeping again. "I've been thinking about that ever since Leon called to tell me what happened. There were a lot of people angry at the Rabbi for different reasons, myself included, but angry to the point of killing him, I can't imagine who would do that."

"Why were people angry at him?"

"Oh," Deborah sighed. "There's no way I can give you a crash course on synagogue politics. It's just too involved."

He smiled, "My wife probably would agree with you, but if I tell you that she, too, is active in our synagogue, and a board member of Gates of Zion in Huntington, Mrs. Katzman, would you think maybe there's still some hope for me?" he was smiling.

"With a name like Brody you're Jewish?"

"Yes, I am," and so was my mother and father, even my grandparents— I hear that back in biblical days there was a little fooling around among the tribes, but in recent years, as far as I know, we're pure. So, try me, maybe I know a little something about the politics you're talking about."

Deborah smiled. She associated with very few people who had a sense of humor, especially since taking over as President of the synagogue, and she wasn't sure exactly how to handle Detective Brody, but she replied, "I think the simplest way I can put it is that as he grew older, the Rabbi's inclination towards traditional Judaism had become more pronounced, and this was causing a lot of controversy in the synagogue, which in turn has had the effect of dividing the membership into various factions, most of whom believed they were angry with the Rabbi for very specific reasons, but in reality it all had to do with his inability to tolerate any deviation from what he deemed to be acceptable Jewish observance."

Now it was Detective Brody's turn to be surprised. "In the Jewish world here in New York, Rabbi Levinson has the reputation of being a giant among men, another King Solomon, maybe even a Jewish 'Saint,' if you'll excuse the expression. It's strange that he would be having so many problems here in his own synagogue."

"For many years Rabbi Levinson was considered, as you put it, another King Solomon here at Beth Torah, too. In fact, I would imagine we have many inactive members who still feel that way about him. But recently he had moved so far to the right in his daily observance of ritual that he began to exasperate some of us who loved him the most. There are members of our Young Couples Club, the YCC, who are even discussing the possibility of starting a new synagogue. Of course, from what I've read, there are some modern scholars who even question King Solomon's judgment."

"Of course," Detective Brody smiled. "Two Jews, three *shuls*. What else is new?"

Deborah snapped back, "In my lifetime, Detective, I've seen with my own eyes what the world can do to Jews. I would hope that at least amongst ourselves we can learn to have some tolerance for differences."

"I'm sorry, I didn't mean to offend you. I know you're very upset at the moment. It's just that what you are describing is so typical. It's how most new *shuls* get built, I suppose."

"Perhaps you're right, but no one ever thought it would happen here. At Beth Torah, we were one big, happy family." Deborah spoke almost in a whisper. "This change is really awful. Our Rabbi was a wonderful man. It's hard to understand how he could have become so oblivious to the feelings of those of us who loved him the most. He had begun to drive everybody who had any contact with him away. It was causing terrible friction among our members."

"Congregational families are like that, Mrs. Katzman. When it's good, it's very good, and when things go bad, the fight gets unbelievably passionate and dirty. Perfectly normal people go berserk when they start talking about their synagogues and their Rabbis. Perhaps when people think God is involved, they don't want to compromise on their convictions."

"Perhaps," she agreed.

"Can you give me the names of some people I can speak with, maybe? Tell me who the players are?"

"Of course," she sighed, "but is it possible for me to have some time to reflect on it? I'm just feeling so drained at the moment. I don't even know if I can think clearly."

"Oh sure," he replied, "I'm sorry. I know this is difficult for you, ma'am. Why don't you get some rest. Think about it and I can speak to you again tomorrow morning. In the meantime, we're checking to see if there are any prints on the gun. You know, all of the obvious kind of stuff."

"Do you really expect to find fingerprints on the gun?"

"No, but we always try. Sometimes we get lucky, you can't overlook the obvious, you know how these things are."

"Of course. Thank you, Detective. I appreciate your courtesy."

"Goodbye, ma'am. Thank you for your time." He got up, strolled over to the door and let himself out of her office

Her secretary buzzed again.

"This guy from *Newsday* is getting impatient. What do you want me to tell him?"

"Tell him I'll just be one more minute. I want to call the synagogue and find out exactly what happened before I speak to him," Deborah replied.

Deborah called the synagogue to speak to Leon Feldman.

"Okay, Leon," she said brusquely, without going through any amenities, "I'm very confused. I was sure you told me the Rabbi was in his study when he got shot."

She waited for his response.

"Oh, no, I was so mixed up when I spoke to you, maybe I didn't make myself clear. The Rabbi was working in the library. The Retirement Club was having breakfast here this morning at 9:00, so I got in early to make sure the bagels had arrived and everything was ready. The Rabbi was supposed to be doing some Torah study with them, so he was here too, I guess, preparing."

"Oh, I forgot about the breakfast," Deborah grumbled. "There's just too much to keep track of."

"You should have seen what was going on with these women. The ambulance drove up just about the time people started arriving for the breakfast, talk about chaos! I've never seen anything to compare to it, even here!"

Leon could be very abrasive at times and there were many congregants who constantly complained about him, but with the Rabbi's help he managed to survive, and now that he had been there for twenty years, firing him didn't seem like the "Judaic" thing to do.

"Some of these older ladies were so hysterical they couldn't even talk," Leon went on. "The minute they realized who was on that stretcher, they began falling down like flies. They were shrieking and falling, shrieking and falling. There were wall-to-wall bodies all over the damn place. The hallway looked like the emergency room at a psychiatric ward. Coffee got spilled all over the new carpet. We'll probably never get it really clean again."

"It sounds horrible, " Deborah sympathized, "but let's get back on target here, for a minute. You were saying that the Rabbi was not in his study, so where was he?"

"Well," he continued, "I heard someone walking down the steps, so I went to see who it was and it was the Rabbi. He told me he was going to use the library in the basement. And, then, just a little while later I heard a loud noise, like a shot, maybe two shots coming from downstairs, and I went running down and there he was slumped over the table in the library moaning. It was a horrible sight."

"Did you see anybody when you got downstairs?" she asked.

"No, I didn't look. The first thing I did was run over to where the Rabbi was, and he seemed like he was trying to say something. I finally realized that he was asking for Esther. I was surprised that he could still actually speak, but he just kept calling her. It was pathetic. I phoned the house but she had already left, so I called her office and left an urgent message for her to contact me.

I think maybe before I did that I called 911. It's just one big blur in my mind. That's all I know."

"You didn't see anyone leave the building?" she asked.

"No, I didn't. I looked, but you know, the basement door was open. Whoever it was must have left in a hurry without ever being noticed. But I'll tell you, I'm willing to bet it's someone in the YCC; those obnoxious, spoiled brats have been out to get him ever since they formed that lousy club."

"There were plenty of other people upset with him too, that doesn't mean anyone at the synagogue wanted to murder him. It's a big leap between being angry with someone and actually shooting them. At least I would like to think so."

"Years ago, maybe, but things have changed. Come on Deborah, people solve everything with a gun, you know that. It's the way things happen nowadays. You say 'No,' and it's 'Up yours, baby,' and boom, boom, they're all gone!"

Given the present set of circumstances, Deborah found Leon's customary crudeness very offensive. Before becoming a Temple administrator at Beth Torah he had been a partner in an over-the-counter brokerage firm that was put out of business by some scandal uncovered by the Securities and Exchange Commission. Although he rarely alluded to that time of his life, older congregants were quick to bring it up. Many of them felt that he was a man not to be trusted, who was too coarse for *"The* Synagogue"; but his survival at Beth Torah was in large part due to Rabbi Levinson, who trusted him and protected him from those who might choose to replace him.

Leon, in turn, had been extraordinarily protective of the Rabbi, particularly in recent years, in large part insulating him from the fairly new and increasingly louder complaints coming from the ranks of Beth Torah's disgruntled population.

The intercom buzzed once again.

"Deborah, this guy from *Newsday* is getting really antsy at this point. I think you'd better speak to him."

"Okay, I think I'm ready," she answered. "Leon, I'll speak to you later, *Newsday* is here."

"Oh, God. Be careful of what you tell them. These weasels twist everything around. They're just trying to sell papers."

"I'm a lawyer, remember? I'm an expert at saying nothing. Bye."

That evening the headline in Newsday read: "'Synagogue Devastated by Murder of Beloved Rabbi,' Cries Frantic Temple Prez."

Chapter Seven

1940

D eborah Benowitz was born in Warsaw, Poland in 1938. Her parents were young and high spirited. According to her mother, her father, Izzy, had been a teacher, a learned and sensitive man with "a quick mind and a gentle manner." He taught music history at the Institute for Jewish Studies and by avocation he, himself, was a musician, a pianist. Her mother played the violin, and together her parents were part of a flourishing, culturally rich lifestyle, somewhat protected from the anti-Semitism, both latent and overt, that surrounded them. When their world began to collapse, both her parents became active in the underground movement and by necessity rather than choice, found themselves living as partisans.

"Your father worked hard to save the children of the ghetto. When everyone was sleeping he would bring them one by one to a small group of people who hid them by day and through the dark of night carried them out of the country and away from Nazi soldiers. Even in the midst of all the horror, there still was an underground chain of courageous, honorable men and women who managed to not get swept up in the madness that surrounded us and devoured the very air we breathed. Can you imagine," her mother would weep, "that these strangers risked their own lives to save a few Jewish children? If only there had been more of them!

"We had an escape plan, but it was always only one more night and only one more little boy or girl that needed his help, and then we too would escape. But we waited one night too many, your father and I, and then they took us to Treblinka. He was a wonderful man, Deborah, you should always be very proud of him. He saved many Jewish lives. He was a true hero."

Deborah had been one of those children who escaped through the "dark of night." Since she was less than three years old at the time, her memories could not be trusted. And yet, there are events in one's life that are so horrifying that they transcend age and become impossible to forget. Over a lifetime, Deborah had never forgotten the stale smell of the couple who carried her for what seemed like an eternity over the rough terrain, until they at last arrived at the body of water that had been their destination. As newlyweds she and Carl had once rented a cabin in Maine from the parents of friends. The cabin had been locked up for several months before they arrived. Carl unlocked the door, and the moment he did Deborah began to shiver uncontrollably. She was immediately paralyzed by fear, and she stood frozen in place, unable to walk through the door—there was the smell, the same stale smell that had carried her to safety through the obscure, Polish terrain. It was more than twenty-five years later, and still she remembered!

She cried herself to sleep that night in Carl's arms. He wanted to comfort her, but he didn't really understand. They both knew from the questions he asked, and the answers she was unable to give, that he could never comprehend the horror of it all. This is the part of her life they could never share. It belonged to Deborah and her mother and the father she no longer remembered, a nightmare from which she would never completely recover. The nightmare that would keep Deborah and Brina Benowitz firmly bonded forever.

Deborah had a vague memory of her mother explaining to her that friends of her father's would be bringing her to visit her Aunt Rose and Uncle Jacob in England. She remembered clearly holding on to her mother's coat, not wanting to leave; but somehow sensing the danger that loomed in front of them all, she had finally allowed herself to be led away, frightened enough to follow any and all instructions, especially when she was told not to speak, because she was much too fearful to utter a word.

Never would she forget the abject terror that overpowered her during those few days of her young life.

Deborah could remember lying on a cot in the hole of a ship. The couple who brought her to the dock pinned a note to her dress and entrusted her to a man with a mustache who wore a blue sailor's hat and pea coat. He smelled of fish, but he had a broad smile and Deborah had a vague memory of his doing magic tricks with a rope that he carried in his pocket. Her memory of the boat ride was dim, but she could still focus in clearly on her Aunt Rose and Uncle Jake greeting her at the pier in London. She didn't want to leave the sailor she had come to trust, and she cried when her aunt and uncle carried her off the ship.

"Poor baby," Aunt Rose was sobbing. "Three years old and look what you've lived through. And what will happen to my sister? God, why didn't they leave with us?"

"They thought we were running off and deserting them," Uncle Jake said. "Thank God we did, at least we can save their baby."

Uncle Jake was crying too.

1946

Brina, Deborah's mother, arrived in England after the war, having miraculously survived the death camp. She was a particularly beautiful woman. She had jet-black hair and huge, dark, round, piercing eyes that glistened like two radiant diamonds in the moonlight. Even as she grew older, she had the kind of beauty that turned heads on the street.

It wasn't until Deborah was sixteen and well established in America that she was able to find the courage to ask her mother how she had managed to survive Treblinka while most of their friends and family had been exterminated. Her mother stared straight ahead into space, managing to avoid eye contact, and answered in a voice devoid of all emotion. "There was a group of German soldiers who were good to me. I was good to them, and they saw to it that I had food and that I stayed alive. I had to live for you. I had to live for my baby."

The subject was never discussed again, but in her mind, Deborah conjured up an image of her mother lying on the rocky, sparse ground with grotesque, vulgar men in uniform mounting her naked body, one after the other, over and over again. It was a vision that could never be erased, and there were times when she was alone at night, when Deborah would have to turn her face into her pillow to muffle a scream because she could truly feel her mother's pain.

Deborah always understood that some of her memories might be warped by time and the limited conceptions of a very young child, but they were nevertheless real for her, and these memories did not dim as the years passed by.

When the war was over, her mother was alive and her father had died attempting to escape from the camp, or so she was told. On the very many occasions when Deborah was alone, she would weep out loud, not understanding why her father had stayed behind to help strange children rather than attempting to escape himself, and why he hadn't seen to it that her mother also escaped to England. At least then she might have been able to avoid the sexual brutality that she was forced to endure in Treblinka.

1949

Deborah was ten years old when she arrived in America with her mother. As had happened previously, Aunt Rose and Uncle Jake came first to scout out the territory. They were both working in factories in the garment district. They wrote wonderful letters about the opportunities for Jewish people in the United States, and her mother was lonely and longing to join them. It didn't take too many months before Aunt Rose and Uncle Jake sent them money, and they both boarded a ship headed for America. They were huddled together with six other women and three children in a cabin meant to hold three people.

Uncle Jake and Aunt Rose were there to greet them as they came through immigration, only this time, instead of tears there were screams of joy.

"Wait, you'll see, Brina. This really is the land of golden opportunity, the 'goldene medina.'"

Deborah and her mother moved on to the same block as her aunt and uncle in the Brownsville section of Brooklyn, a lower-middle-income neighborhood that housed many other Jewish survivors. For the first year she and her mother lived together in a one-and-a-half-room apartment, over a cleaning store. It was unbearably hot in the summer and cold in the winter, but her mother assured her this apartment was only temporary. They had to be grateful for all that Uncle Jake and Aunt Rose tried to do for them, but as soon as she could get a decent job for herself, they would move.

Deborah's mother also got a job in a factory in the garment district. She was sewing dresses, but with her good looks and genuine charisma she was soon promoted into the front office where she spent much of her time attracting new clients. It was there that she got to know Benjamin Franklin Lieb, one of the company's largest clients. Soon after meeting him her mother changed jobs and was put in charge of Benjamin Lieb's entire showroom operation. At that point she and her mother, along with Aunt Rose and Uncle Jake, purchased a two-family house in Bensonhurst, where there was a cool breeze that came in from the ocean during the summer, and enough heat to keep them warm in the winter.

Brina described Ben Lieb as her "very dear friend." He visited often and brought them both many gifts. Deborah learned very quickly that as soon as she mentioned wanting something, Ben would bring it on his next visit. He would on occasion mention his own two children and talk about the things they did together, but he never brought them to meet her. At first this seemed odd to Deborah, but she didn't spend much time thinking about it. Her mother never cried about the past when Ben was around. In fact, when she was with him she seemed almost happy. For that reason, even when Deborah was old enough to understand the significance of their relationship, she was forgiving of her mother for finding whatever way she could to cope with the tragedy of her life.

Uncle Jake and Aunt Rose never had any children of their own.

"Who could bring a child into such a world," they had told her. "We had you to take care of, and your mother to worry about, there was no extra money for children."

And, so, Deborah lived in the shadow of three doting adults, under-standing that for them she had to achieve everything in life that they were unable to achieve themselves. For her mother, she studied the violin so she could become a musician like her father. She was on the girl's volleyball team in school just so Uncle Jake could watch her compete. Aunt Rose and Uncle Jake took her to *shul* on Saturday mornings. Uncle Jake sat down-stairs and prayed with the men; Deborah and Aunt Rose went upstairs and socialized with the women. Aunt Rose was the Chairwoman of the Synagogue's Ladies Auxiliary, and Deborah enjoyed the fuss the women made over her ability to speak Yiddish and her British accent, but Brina, Deborah's mother, never went to *shul*.

"I looked for God in Poland, I looked for God in Treblinka," she said. "I got tired of looking. Here in America, I have Ben. I don't need God. But you, Deborah, you go and look for yourself. Maybe for you, God will be there."

In the local elementary school in Bensonhurst, and later in junior high, Deborah was always uncomfortable. She never felt as though she belonged. There were girls who she sat with in the lunchroom or played ball with in the gym, but no one who she ever associated with after school. The other children were happy and untroubled. Deborah never told any-one about her past and she never complained about her discomfort with the present. If she was asked about her father, she had learned to say that he died in the war. No one had ever asked for any more explanation than that. Many soldiers had died fighting the Nazis. From her distinctly British accent everyone, including her teachers, assumed she had been born in Britain. She was described as intelligent, shy, and well mannered.

Deborah was tall and thin. She knew her arms were too long for her body and her body was too short for her legs. She never understood how her mother could be so beautiful and she so awkward in appearance.

"You look just like your father," Aunt Rose and Uncle Jake would tell her. "It's uncanny how much you look like Izzy. You're his spitting image."

Of course she had no memory of what her father looked like, just shadows from the past that floated in and out of her mind fleetingly on those occasions when she was left alone with only the phantom of obscure memories to keep her company, and there was not one photo that survived for her to look at. So she believed Aunt Rose and Uncle Jake when they told her she looked like her father, but she still prayed that one day she would wake up, look in the mirror, and find that, magically, she had become beautiful, like her mother.

When it was time to go to high school, Deborah applied to and was accepted into the High School of Music and Art in Upper Manhattan. She traveled two hours each way to attend that school, and she traveled alone since she was the only student commuting from Bensonhurst, but Deborah knew her mother would be thrilled to see her studying with real musicians, and making her mother happy took precedence over everything else at that point in her life.

Her high school years continued to be lonely ones. She displayed considerable musical ability, no doubt part of her mother and father's legacy, and even in a high school filled with talented musicians Deborah distinguished herself as one of the most gifted in her class. While she no longer felt like a misfit, there was never a time when she was completely comfortable among her peers. She joined a string quartet, but it was primarily to give her mother pleasure, rather than for her own enjoyment, and when it came time to graduate Deborah was confused about her future.

She wanted to go to Hunter College in Manhattan. It was free, and it was an all-girls' college. Deborah was quite sure she would be more comfortable if she didn't have the opposite sex to worry about. She was five-nine, and she felt big and clumsy next to the boys in her classes. She was seventeen and still had never been on a date of any kind. Ben was willing to pay for her to go to any college she chose, but Deborah wouldn't let him.

"Why don't you let Ben do things for you?" her mother sighed.

"I want to go to a girls' college. Hunter is a great school. There is no reason for Ben to spend a lot of money.

"Barnard is better," her mother had insisted.

"That's not true, and I want to go to Hunter."

Hunter College had proven to be a wise decision. Being in an all-girls' school had allowed her to expand her interests and to feel more comfortable with the other students. For the first time in her life she made friends and began to have a social life away from her family. Her grades were excellent and her advisors encouraged her to seek out a profession rather than going to college to find a husband as so many other girls in her class chose to do.

"Law school? Whoever heard of a girl going to law school?" Uncle Jake was shocked. "Why don't you become a teacher, then you'll be able to have a steady job with good hours; you'll have your summers free, and some day when you have children, you'll be able to come home early from school to be with them."

"I don't want to be a teacher, Uncle Jake. I want to be a lawyer."

If Deborah had learned anything from watching her mother, it was that she had to be able to support herself. Teachers did not earn very much money; lawyers did. What if she never got married? Four years of college and she had still never had a real date. When she put on high heels she was taller than most of the young men she came into contact with. She had several men friends, but no boyfriends.

"Stand up straight and be proud," her mother would say. "There is a tall man out there looking for someone your size, and if you're all stooped over, he's not going to find you."

Deborah knew her mother was shrewd enough to have learned to use her beauty and sensuality for survival. She knew she had neither her mother's beauty nor her sensuality; if she was ever to survive it would have to be through her wits, and for that she needed a profession, one that would bring her respect, as well as the ability to earn enough money to live on.

"I never heard of a lady lawyer, darling, but if that's what you want, Ben says he will pay for it. You go to any school you want."

"I don't know why you want to be a lawyer, but you're like my own child, and if that's what you want, of course I'll pay for it," Ben assured her. "You don't have to worry about anything."

The only thing Deborah's mother liked about law school was the male-to-female ratio.

"One girl to all boys, now that's a change for the better," her mother asserted. "Maybe here you'll even find a husband."

41

Chapter Eight

1988

The headline in the local newspaper read: "Civil Rights Rabbi from Beth Torah Elected President of ZOA."

Rabbi Levinson was the newly elected President of the Zionist Organization of America. He was revered by his colleagues and counterparts in other congregations, who spoke often about his never-ending energy and commitment. He was affectionately known among them as "*The* Rabbi from *The* Synagogue," the man whose congregation virtually gave him anything he wanted and who apparently could do no wrong. Rabbi Levinson was also the highest-paid Conservative Rabbi on the East Coast. His salary was spoken about in jealous whispers by others who wanted desperately to emulate him. Most were jealous!

Over the years everyone, even those who hired Rabbi Levinson, had lost track of the liberal views that had attracted them to him originally. In fact, as time went on Rabbi Levinson had become more and more conservative in his convictions, most particularly with those involving Jewish practice and customs. Nevertheless, even if he had grown to be politically to the right of his congregants, Rabbi Levinson had participated in so many life-cycle events over the years that it was hard to find a family that he hadn't touched through the death of a parent, the birth of a baby, a Bar Mitzvah, or the marriage of a child.

"Like Jacob's ladder that connected him to heaven, there's a cord that connects me to my congregants," Rabbi Levinson would often say. "A cord that binds us closely together into one Jewish community."

Over these many years, his oratory ability had become ever more inspirational. So spellbinding were his sermons that even those who disagreed with him the most vehemently would faithfully come to hear what he had to say. It was true that Rabbi Levinson was dearly loved and much respected by his congregants, in spite of his politics or the narrowness with which he viewed and interpreted the Torah.

Chapter Nine

E sther Levinson had become a well-known person in her own right.
She headed a special Children's Task Force called "Children at Risk
Educationally," most often referred to by the acronym CARE. The task
force was begun by Mayor Koch and continued by those who followed
him. Esther's most important function as the Task Force Chairperson was
to attract private money to direct and support a group of impoverished
children whose superior intelligence or special talents caused them to stand
out from their peers. Her program was so successful that it became the
prototype around the country of how the private sector could be utilized to
augment public education.

Being the wife of such a well-known Rabbi gave Esther a unique status
within certain charitable institutions which enabled her to approach people
who might otherwise be inaccessible for donations.

"Does your husband object to your tapping his sources for funds?" her
colleagues would ask?

"Why should he mind?" she would reply. "The donors are going to
give to more than Jewish institutions. All I do is show them a way to direct
their funds. No, Saul doesn't seem to mind."

Esther freely admitted that she delighted in the extra strength her husband's position afforded her to carry out her job more successfully. Her task,
after all, was so selfless that she was compelled to use whatever means she had
at her disposal to help as many of "her children," these "Special Children of
God," as she could, and she always referred to them as "My children."

Saul and Esther had reached an unspoken compromise over the years. They never criticized each other in front of others and publicly they always appeared to be completely in sync. If individual convictions prevented one of them from giving the other overt support, they would not say anything that could be interpreted as disagreement. At charitable parties that required one or the other's attendance, the Rabbi and his wife always sat with the UJA/Federation delegation. That was where Saul was most comfortable, and where Esther was free to do some of her most successful networking.

Rabbi Levinson kept himself in shape by playing tennis with many of his congregants. His day was a long one; nevertheless, he played tennis three to four days a week. He may not have been invited to join the golf club in Green County, but here on the north shore of Long Island every tennis club within the reach of Beth Torah had extended an open invitation to Rabbi Levinson to come whenever and as often as he would like, and he did.

Rabbi Levinson's hair was still full and as white as snow, and his skin had aged well. In fact, the Rabbi was a better-looking man at sixty than he had been at thirty. There were certain widows and divorcees within the Beth Torah family who were not beyond flirting with him from time to time, but it was all in good fun since everyone knew that a man as pious as their Rabbi would never be one to succumb to such earthly pleasures.

Grandpa Levinson had continued to be Rabbi Saul's mentor. They spoke often, and although he was quite old at this point, Saul valued his counsel. When Grandpa suffered his stroke in 1988, Saul spent as many hours as he could at the hospital with him, holding his hand and listening to the radio, the way they did during those early years in Brooklyn.

"If your grandmother were alive, she would have a brew to make this arm move again," Grandpa would exclaim.

"Absolutely, she would," Saul agreed, while his father, the doctor, stayed in the background, rolling his eyes in agony over what he was hearing.

1990

With all of the compromises Esther Levinson had been forced to make in her marriage, the only one that she gradually began to find almost insufferable to live with was what she perceived to be her husband's exacerbating intolerance. According to the *New York Times*, Grandpa Levinson died peacefully in his sleep with his grandson, Rabbi Saul Levinson, at his side. But Esther knew better; she alone understood that Grandpa Levinson had actually never died at all, for on the day of his passing, his essence was reborn and destined to live on in his grandson Saul. She sat by and watched while with each passing day, Saul became more and more traditional in his religious fervor. In fact, Grandpa's passing was the first of two points in time that Esther could single out as being the most important moments when things at Beth Torah began to change.

There was a time early in their marriage when she had been able to influence Saul's thinking and direct him towards a more cosmopolitan point of view; but this was no longer possible, and while he dutifully accompanied her to events that were important to her own career, he had begun to evidence disdain for anything that wasn't clearly related to Israel or the plight of Jewish peoplehood. Esther would point to opinions expressed by several of his more liberal colleagues in Manhattan as worthy of admiration.

"Those are your values, not mine," he would respond. "I have my own role models, and they don't include men who would defile our traditions."

Esther and Saul still enjoyed a satisfying sexual relationship, although the frequency of their coming together had certainly diminished over time. Actually, once Esther realized that she was destined not to have a child of her own, their physical relationship became much more open and enjoyable, and was one of the few common bonds they had to link them together.

In 1991, the week following the High Holy Days, a delegation of women active in the Young Couples Club came to visit with Rabbi Levinson.

The spokesperson for the group was a young woman named Joyce Kaplan. She was the daughter of Norman and Estelle Gross, a very successful real estate family who had personally underwritten the refurbishing of the sanctuary, and who had always been particularly generous to the Rabbi's Discretionary Fund. Joyce was a graduate of Columbia Teachers College and she volunteered several days a week as an assistant in the synagogue's nursery school. Her husband, Fred Kaplan, was now a partner in her father's business. She undoubtedly had been chosen to speak because of her family's warm relationship with the Rabbi.

"Rabbi Levinson, we can't help but notice that many Conservative congregations have begun to count women in their daily *minyan*, and we were wondering if the Ritual Committee could take this matter up to study this year to see if we can make this happen at Beth Torah."

"This is not a decision for the Ritual Committee," he quickly responded. "This is a rabbinical decision."

"Well, then," she went on, completely undeterred by his answer, "perhaps those of us who are interested can study the matter with you."

"Since when would I refuse anyone an opportunity to study? We can study every day if you'd like, but I have to tell you that on this issue the '*halachah*,' that is Jewish law, is clear: women are welcome to come and pray and observe, but they cannot read from the Torah at *Shabbos* services, and without ten men, we don't have a *minyan*."

"If it's so clear, Rabbi, how come other Conservative synagogues are doing it differently?"

"Joyce, I've known you since you were a little girl, and what have I taught you? I can only do what I know is Judaically kosher and hope that others will follow my lead. I can't be responsible for what other Rabbis are doing. You come and pray at our *minyan*, and I, personally, will welcome you."

"As long as there are ten men along with me, Rabbi?"

"Of course there have to be ten men with you."

"That's not fair, Rabbi. It's just not fair."

"No, it's more than fair. These rules were made to protect women and make it possible for them to be able to care for their children. The burden is on men because for them daily prayer is mandated. They have to leave whatever they're doing to get to a *minyan*. Our laws understand that a woman caring for a baby can't just drop everything and go to a *minyan*. You should be happy that you are being given a reprieve in deference to your duty to your family."

"I have a maid to take care of my children for that one hour, Rabbi, and if it's so hard for my husband to get there, I should be able to go in his place."

"That's just not the way it is. Come every day, I'd love to see you—I'd love to see all of you women there, but with you we need ten men."

Esther wasn't especially surprised to hear Saul describe this encounter. In a community like theirs it was just a matter of time until the equality issue would have had to become a cause célèbre. She was actually amazed it hadn't happened earlier. It obviously was a sign of people's reluctance to go against their Rabbi's convictions.

"Saul, maybe you were too condescending to these women; maybe you should have offered to study with them, and through study try to bring them around to your way of thinking," Esther said, choosing her words carefully.

"In this world there are knowledgeable people and they're the ones who make decisions. You don't have one of your homeless Christians coming in to tell you how to get donations from Jewish businessmen, and I don't need a congregant who doesn't even keep a kosher home coming in to tell me who to count in a *minyan*."

"Yes, but Saul, I listen. You have to listen. Joyce Kaplan's family has a lot of influence."

"More influence than me maybe, you think? You think that my followers are going to allow some supermarket developer to dictate God's laws in my sanctuary? If that's what you think, Esther, then you're not listening to what my congregants are telling me."

Saul's face was purple with rage, and his outburst startled her, but it was only the first of many such moments yet to come. Ever since Grandpa's death Esther had lost all of her ability to influence Saul's religious fervor, but it was this night that Esther had clearly imprinted in her mind as the precise moment in time that the cord that bound Rabbi Saul Levinson to his congregation began to fray.

Chapter Ten

June 1992

T he local newspaper headline read: "Bankruptcy Lawyer Elected First Woman Prez of Synagogue Beth Torah."

Deborah had taken over as President of Beth Torah on June 1st, the beginning of the synagogue's fiscal year. Her first request for a meeting had come from Joyce Kaplan who wished to speak to her on behalf of the Young Couples Club. Joyce arrived together with another officer of the YCC, Rita Calderon. Rita was a Sephardic Jew, and clearly one of the sexier young women in the community, both in and out of the synagogue. She had very fair skin, and long jet-black hair permmed to hang down her back and around her face in ringlets. She had almond-shaped brown eyes and full, perfectly molded lips. No matter what she wore, all of her clothing was carefully selected to emphasize her slim waist and large breasts. Her cleavage was spectacular!

Rita Calderon's husband was a popular matrimonial attorney and, like his wife, he too was extraordinarily good to look at. Lester Calderon was tall, with a rugged complexion and dark brown hair. One of the two most striking things about him was his eyes—two rich, deep violet pools of velvet, so penetrating that every woman he looked at felt uncomfortably naked in his presence. The other striking thing about Lester was his physique. He had built an exercise room onto their home as an extension of the master bedroom. There Lester faithfully worked out every day, creating an upper body that was the envy of all the men at their pool and tennis club. During weekends in the summer the men would tease him mercilessly about his Tarzan-like appearance, but the women followed him around waiting for an opportunity to feel his muscle. Lester would strut about in his bikini, with his shoulders tilted back, and his muscles bulging, as if to announce to everyone in view, "Here I am, come and get me, I dare you!"

Clearly, Rita and Lester Calderon were the most beautiful duo around.

"Congratulations, Deborah," Joyce spoke up. "Rita and I wanted to come as representatives of the YCC of Beth Torah to tell you how delighted we all are to have you as our President."

"Thank you. I appreciate everyone's support. This is very new for me and I have a lot to learn. I hope we will all be able to work together."

Joyce smiled, "There's no reason why we can't all work together."

"Of course. We can and should work together," said Rita.

Deborah smiled, "That's great. So, there is nothing special on your minds then?"

"Well, not exactly," Joyce replied. "I do hate to do this to you the first week of your new reign, so to speak, but there is one issue that really has to be addressed very quickly."

"Very quickly," echoed Rita.

Deborah understood the situation well. Over the last two to three years, the Young Couples Club was taken over by an activist group anxious to make changes with regards to various religious practices within the synagogue. They spoke loudly to anyone within the Beth Torah family who would listen to their views on what they considered to be Rabbi Levinson's anti-feminist positions. Deborah understood only too well that if she was ever going to bring any semblance of calm back to Beth Torah, it would have to begin through the auspices of the YCC.

Joyce continued, "Both Rita and I have daughters who will be celebrating their Bat Mitzvahs within the next few years."

Deborah smiled, "Well, *mazel tov*. That's wonderful."

"It could be wonderful, but at the moment it's not so wonderful. Among the seventy-five families who belong to the YCC, fifteen of us have a daughter who will become a Bat Mitzvah within the next two years, and because of our Rabbi, all of these ceremonies will take place on Friday night instead of on Saturday morning."

"I presume you have spoken to Rabbi Levinson about this," Deborah inquired politely.

"Of course we have—more than once. Every other Conservative synagogue in the area is allowing girls to become a Bat Mitzvah on Saturday mornings. This is not an Orthodox *shul*, you know. Rabbi Levinson seems to think that we are in the middle of a European *shtetl* somewhere."

"That's right, a *shtetl*," Rita echoed once again.

Joyce was clearly agitated, Rita was programmed to agree with everything she said, and Deborah needed breathing room.

"Please, this is my first week. I need a little time to look into all of the issues that are out there. Why don't you let me call you as soon as I've had an opportunity to familiarize myself with what's going on."

"That's fine, but we don't have much time, you know. I'm sure you have heard about the group that has gotten together to form a new Reform synagogue here in town." Joyce smiled sadistically as she spoke.

Deborah could feel her stomach muscles tighten up, but she knew it was important to appear calm and composed.

"Just give me some time, Joyce. I'll be back to you very soon, I promise."

Deborah turned abruptly towards Rita, "And, Rita, I have to know your secret, how do you keep yourself in such great shape? I bet you don't have an ounce of fat on your body!"

"God, yes," agreed Joyce. "With a body like that I could learn to hate her. Three children and she's still a size 4!"

Rita giggled with delight.

Deborah was satisfied she had eased the tension a bit. "I'll speak to you both soon."

"Sure. We'll be waiting," Joyce answered.

"Yes, we will be waiting," echoed Rita.

Deborah had a breakfast meeting set up with Rabbi Levinson several days later.

"I realize he's become more traditionally observant in his religious practices over the years," she said to Carl over dinner, "but I still respect Rabbi Levinson as my Rabbi, and I really do like him. I can't help but admire his sincerity and his willingness to stand by his convictions."

"That's why you're a good person for the job," Carl replied. "You've got no axe to grind with him. You'll find a way. You'll settle it just like you do those bankruptcy cases you handle in the office. I have complete confidence in you."

Deborah and Carl had met accidentally, when she was studying to pass the Bar exam. She went to the NYU library each evening to study alone. Deborah had discovered early on that she did her best on exams when she studied by herself. She still lived at home, and her mother or aunt and uncle would constantly disturb her by insisting that she eat or take a break now and then. The library was quiet and open late, and here she was able to study and absorb the many, many facts that were necessary to memorize. Each night, before going into the library, she would stop at a nearby restaurant for a fast dinner to get her through the night. That was where she met Dr. Carl Katzman. He was an internist working at St. Vincent's Hospital. He had an apartment near the law school. At first they simply acknowledged each other going in and out of the restaurant, but gradually Carl became friendlier and soon they began sharing the same table, making casual conversation over dinner.

Deborah was twenty-six and Carl was thirty-five, but somehow that made him appear even more attractive. He was not terribly tall, about her own height, which was acceptable, if not ideal, and their relationship developed bit by bit over the four-month period that Deborah had devoted to studying for the bar exam. When he finally asked her to go to a movie with him she was thrilled, and counted the minutes until their first date.

Carl had a sweetness about him that Deborah had not found in any other man she had ever met. He was fascinated with her family. He had told Deborah how much he adored and admired her mother; he thought Uncle Jake's bad jokes were really funny, and he knew that both Uncle Jake and Aunt Rose were wonderful for all they had done for her over the years. He was grateful to Ben for having helped her through school, but now he wanted to take over from all of them and be the one to look after her for the rest of her life.

Carl was also an only child. His mother had been a World War II widow. His father died in the invasion of Normandy, and he and Deborah discovered they shared many dreams, and had many nightmares in common. However, unlike Deborah, who had felt protected and loved by her family, Carl's mother had been unable to cope. She fell apart after his father's death, and he had become the man of the house at a very early age, taking care of his mother both emotionally and physically until her death from cancer, only several months before meeting Deborah. Deborah Benowitz and Carl Katzman were a perfect fit and they were destined to have a good marriage.

-◆-

"Rabbi, isn't there some way we can work this out?" Deborah pleaded over breakfast. "This is a new generation, and they feel strongly about women's equality."

"And so do I. Does anyone who knows my wife even think that I treat her less than an equal? Not Esther! Anyone who knows her would know how ridiculous this is. However, Jewish law is what it is, and I am hardly in a position to change it."

"But isn't there some basis that allows other Conservative Rabbis to come to different conclusions than you do?" Deborah politely asked.

"You'll have to ask them. For me there is no basis. We read from the Torah on Saturday mornings; in my sanctuary, women don't read from the Torah together with men on *Shabbos*."

"Well, Rabbi, is it possible to have a Bat Mitzvah on Saturday and have somebody else read from the Torah? The girls could read from the Haftorah, and that could be a good compromise."

"Anything is possible, that doesn't mean I am going to allow it to happen here."

"Well, is there any law against that?" Deborah pushed harder.

"The appearance is what we have to be concerned about. You bring a girl up on the bema on a Saturday and right away everyone thinks she's reading from the Torah. I won't allow it. Appearance is important. And another important issue is everyone will be distracted and no one will be doing what they are supposed to be coming here to do—they're supposed to be praying!"

"Well, as far as people being distracted, that may happen the first week or two, but it will clear up just as soon as everyone becomes accustomed to the new practice."

"No, you don't understand, Deborah. Men are the way men are, and having attractive young girls on the bema will undoubtedly divert their attention away from the prayer books. That's human nature and that will not go away."

"Rabbi, I'm not going to push this any further right at this moment, but why don't you take some time and think about it? Look at what's going on around us. Every active member of this synagogue has taken sides and they're all fighting. No one is happy and everyone is diverted from praying.

If there's any way around it, maybe we should consider all the good things that will happen if we do it."

Rabbi Levinson was about to answer her, but Deborah quickly cut him off.

"Please, Rabbi, don't say anything now. Just think about it, and we'll talk again."

❧

"I think you are doing very well for yourself," Simmy Monash told her. "No one new is threatening to quit, Joyce Kaplan believes you're addressing her problems. It's terrific."

Barry Weinstein was agitated, however. "Listen, at some point decisions have to be made. You can only drag this out for so long and then you'll be expected to do something."

"I was hoping the Rabbi might give in on this one," Deborah smiled.

"You can't be for real," Barry sighed. "He'll never give in. He's got three years left on his contract. We can probably work out an early retirement scheme for him after that. He can become Rabbi Emeritus. We'll give him a lot of honors. He'll make plenty of money by performing weddings and funerals. God knows he'll be in demand for speaking engagements around the country, and he'll be thrilled to be able to do and say what he wants."

"I don't know, Barry, I doubt that he wants an early retirement," Deborah replied. "The only sense I can make out of his unwillingness to allow this to happen is his fear of what men will be thinking about by having women on the bema. Well, who knows what they're thinking about anyway? He certainly can't expect to control people's minds! Also, three years is a long time, what do we do in the meantime?" Deborah asked.

"We have to find a way to convince the YCC group to hold the status quo," Barry responded.

"If you hold the status quo, you're going to lose the entire YCC and probably every prospective young person who might consider joining this congregation, along with the older members who are sympathetic to their cause."

Simmy interjected, smiling and touching her hand in a fatherly gesture, "But that's why we've got you. You can make these women understand that three years is not that long to wait."

"Simmy," Deborah was quick to respond, "I may have been elected President of the synagogue, but the job doesn't come with the power to perform miracles. You should all be very clear that something has to change. I'm not exactly sure of what, but there has to be at least the illusion that the leadership of this synagogue is listening and willing to take some suggestions or a large segment of our younger membership is going to leave to help start a new synagogue, and nothing we do is going to work."

"Illusion is fine. We can have all the illusion you want. I don't think the Rabbi cares much about illusions. But for a man like this, we have to have respect. In my country this couldn't happen."

"I'm sick of hearing about your country. In your country, you would have been hung years ago," Rochelle Levy interrupted. "Deborah is right. These young people need to be given at least a small amount of credence. You're not the only one who loves the Rabbi, Simmy, but we all have to come up with something that he is willing to do that will calm things down. Don't you think so, Harry?"

Harry looked up from his newspaper and gazed tenderly in his wife's direction, "If Rochelle says so, it's got to be the right thing to do, no question about it."

Deborah interrupted. "Well, we can have the *B'not Mitzvah* on Saturday and have the Rabbi or the Cantor do the Torah reading. The girls can read the Haftorah. It's being done in other places, I understand."

"That we can forget about—he'll never do it," Barry said, sounding despondent.

"There's no end to this. I can't stand it anymore," Rochelle cried. "It's no pleasure to come here these days, you know? Do you have any idea what Sisterhood meetings are like? You've got the younger women attacking, the older women defending. Whoever thought this could happen at *The* Synagogue? Harry and I are just sick over what's going on here. Isn't that right, Harry?"

"Sick, Rochelle, just sick. This used to be a quiet peaceful *shul*; I can't believe what's going on here. You all just listen to Rochelle, she knows what she is talking about. Listen to her and you won't go wrong."

Simmy Monash mumbled in his mother tongue. No one understood what he was saying.

❧

Norman Gross, Joyce Kaplan's father, had always been a fair man, an easy touch for a donation and someone the synagogue could always count on for strong support. When he called Deborah to set up a meeting, she assumed he wanted to speak about the same issues that concerned his daughter. She wasn't surprised to see him walk into the synagogue together with his son-in-law, Fred Kaplan, to keep their appointment. They met in the library.

Deborah greeted them warmly, "I'm delighted to see you. Norman, you look wonderful."

Norman Gross was over six feet tall. He had broad shoulders and a full head of gray hair that was carefully blown into place. Deborah noted that his body was lean, with no excess fat. He looked amazingly young for someone who had to be pushing at least seventy. "And it's always a pleasure to see you," he answered, sounding very sincere. "How is Carl? I haven't seen him at the tennis club lately."

"Oh, he's busy, I guess, but with the boys out of the house, we try to do things together when we can, and I don't play tennis, so . . ."

Norman Gross smiled. "I presume you know my son-in-law, Fred Kaplan," he went on.

Deborah held out her hand. "Actually, I've seen him around. I've seen him called to the Torah as a *Kohane*, but I don't know that we've ever formally met. You know, before we even begin to chat, I want to assure you both that I am having dialogues with the Rabbi and my executive board, and we are trying to come to some compromise that will address all of the YCC's issues."

"That's wonderful; I'm glad to hear that," Fred Kaplan answered, smiling as warmly as his father-in-law. Fred was shorter than his father-in-law, and stocky, just the slightest bit overweight. He had a round face, with straight brown hair.

"Deborah, believe me, that's not what we're here about," Norman quickly responded.

"Well, I'm all ears," she said, instantly distressed to realize she was about to be presented with yet another problem.

"To get right to the point, let's talk *tachlis*. I'm sure you know that our company owns the land across the road from the synagogue." Norman's whole demeanor changed as he spoke. He was clearly ready to get down to business.

"Do you mean the parking lot?" she asked.

"Well, let's say it's the property that I have allowed our congregation to use as a parking lot since almost forever. It's actually property that I could have developed many times, but I haven't only because of my devotion to this congregation. There was a lot of money to be made from that property.

I knew Rabbi Levinson didn't want us parking at the synagogue on *Shabbos* and other holidays, and since we're in a somewhat isolated location, many of our members would have great difficulty coming to *shul* if there was no place they could park, so I put down some concrete and everyone in the congregation has been parking there for years."

Norman Gross was beaming with pride. His son-in-law nodded in agreement.

"I think everyone is aware that that property belongs to you, and we're grateful. It's certainly a very wonderful thing that you have been doing for your synagogue, but knowing you, Norman, it's not surprising that you would be so generous." Deborah couldn't believe it was she speaking. Maybe when she was finished with the Temple presidency she could become a career diplomat.

"Well, are you aware that a handful of old men who recently moved into the new retirement village in town are upset that I have made it possible for our members to drive their cars here to pray on Saturday?"

"No, I can't say that I am," answered Deborah. "I know we have very few men attending services from that retirement community altogether. One of my colleagues is the lawyer who represents the retirement home where they live. They have their own daily services and they really don't need us," she went on, still trying to grasp what the problem was.

"Well, there's about a half dozen of them who have begun to come to our weekday *minyan,* and they are now showing up on Saturdays too, and they have complained to the Rabbi about the parking lot. They want me to close it down."

"That's absurd, and anyway it's none of their business. I doubt that they're even members."

The two men were obviously pleased to hear her response. "That's exactly the point, but the Rabbi agrees with them."

"I can't believe that," Deborah was no longer smiling. "We're not an Orthodox congregation, and most of us do not live within walking distance. We have to have a place to park or even people like me will stop coming. It's impossible! Rabbi Levinson wouldn't go along with something this ridiculous. I don't believe it."

"Well, you see, that just doesn't seem to be true," Fred interjected.

"Listen, I'm new at this job, so why don't you spell it out for me. Why would the Rabbi possibly want to keep his own congregants out of the synagogue? To me, it is just illogical."

"It's quite simple," Fred picked up the conversation. "With these six men, the Rabbi has no problem getting his daily *minyan,* without them there are many days when he doesn't have ten men. The Rabbi, as you know, has become more concerned about his *minyan* in recent years. It's very important to him, so he wants us to block off the parking lot on *Shabbos* and make these guys happy."

Deborah stared at them in disbelief. "He told you this?" she asked.

"He called me yesterday," Norman Gross stated candidly.

"How does the Rabbi expect people to get here then? He can't expect people to walk five to ten miles on a Saturday morning." Deborah was still certain there had to be some misunderstanding.

"According to our Rabbi, they can walk or leave their cars in town and take a taxi." Norman Gross wasn't smiling.

"Of course," Fred blurted out sarcastically, "we actually do have more than ten people attending the minyan every day, it's just that according to our Rabbi, some of them are not worthy of being counted. Some of Joyce's friends have suggested we use the property that the parking lot is on to build a Reform synagogue. It's certainly a thought worth considering."

Norman Gross jumped up, obviously irritated, "Fred, just stop it. This is not what we're here to talk about." He turned to Deborah, "I am sorry. I want you to understand that this man-woman issue may be important to my daughter and son-in-law. Where I come from, it's up to a Rabbi to decide who belongs in a *minyan.* I'm not interfering with that, and believe me, the last thing I ever want to do is split *The* Synagogue into two parts. I just want to know who the hell these people are who think they can come in, not even bother to pay dues and join, and suddenly they're telling me that what I've been doing all these years is wrong! I'm not a *goy*? If there's been no problem with the parking lot until now, then there should be no problem going forward."

Deborah didn't know what to say. "Norman, why don't you let me speak to the Rabbi and find out what all this is about. It's not that I don't believe you, it's just that the whole concept is hard for me to understand. I'll call you tomorrow, I promise."

"You don't have to promise. You say you'll call, I know you'll call. I don't know you just from yesterday after all. This synagogue is a part of me; I love this place, it's like home. We just don't need strangers coming in here from nowhere and taking over. I'll wait for your call." He motioned to Fred who stood up, waved goodbye, and followed his father-in-law down the hallway to the entrance of the building.

Deborah ran home to call Barry, Simmy, and Rochelle.

"Rabbi, we have to talk," Deborah asserted, walking into his office at 8:30 the next morning.

"Usually even the President asks for an appointment," Rabbi Levinson answered, with just the slightest bit of sarcasm in his voice. "Barbara Goldberg's mother died. I'm preparing for the funeral this morning and I don't have much time. However, come in, for the President I can always manage a few minutes."

"I'm due in court in less than an hour, so I'll make this as fast and as direct as I can, Rabbi. Norman Gross and Fred Kaplan met with me last night. They insist that you told them to block off the parking lot they own from now on on Shabbos," she stated candidly.

"Yes. So?" he asked.

"You mean it's true?" Deborah's anxiety was obvious.

"Well, you know that on Saturday we really shouldn't have people driving up and parking right across the street from the *shul,* and in a parking lot run by one of our members yet, it just isn't the right thing to do."

"If it's been all right to do that for twenty-five years, what's wrong with doing it now?" she asked very politely, trying hard to control her temper.

"We have begun to attract some more observant Jews from the retirement village. They object to it, and I believe they're correct," he explained.

"This is not an Orthodox congregation, Rabbi, and that parking lot does not belong to the synagogue. Norman Gross has been kind enough to let us use it all of these years; he is *not* going to block it off on *Shabbos.*" Deborah was astounded at her own reaction. She was actually standing up to the Rabbi in a fashion she would never have thought possible just a few weeks earlier.

"Deborah, really. Calm down. There is no reason why people can't walk on Saturday. It's healthier for them, they'll get some exercise."

Deborah raised her voice just enough to demonstrate her outrage. "If someone wants exercise, they'll walk, but most of us are not walking. Rabbi, I'm saying it again, we are not Orthodox here at Beth Torah, and no one should be compelled to walk if they don't want to. It's not going to happen, Rabbi. Believe me, it's not!"

"If they don't want to walk they can take the car service from the railroad station. There's no problem."

"Surely you understand, Rabbi, that Norman Gross is our largest contributor. Even more important than that, he's a good man. He deserves your respect and your support. He is feeling very unappreciated at the moment, and I don't believe we should allow that to happen."

"I had hoped things would be different with you as President, Deborah. I can see they're not. Everything in the synagogue cannot revolve around money. These men from the retirement village are pious, learned men. I have been studying with them several times a week. We need them to make our *minyan* on many mornings, and they too should be respected," the Rabbi stubbornly persisted. "I don't see the likes of Norman Gross at our weekday *minyan*, you know."

"He works in Manhattan. How do you know he's not attending a *minyan* there? On this one, Rabbi, you're not going to win. Norman Gross, in his own way, is also a pious, learned man. He owns the parking lot. It is his, not yours, and I am going to tell him not to block it off, regardless of what you say. Don't you understand that our younger members, probably ninety percent of the YCC, are looking for property in order to build another synagogue? If I leave it in your hands they will be putting their cornerstone into that parking lot, and before we know it, we could lose the entire congregation."

The Rabbi appeared more weary than angry. "Don't you think you are being just a little melodramatic," he sighed.

"No, Rabbi, this is what is real. This is what is going on. It's not a nightmare that is going away in the morning, and, Rabbi, this will not happen while I'm president, that's not how I choose to be remembered. I'll have to call an emergency board meeting, but, please, Rabbi, I am pleading with you: these men are total strangers, and they're not members; you can't allow them to dictate what our congregants should be doing."

Rabbi Levinson turned his back to her and returned to reading the papers on his desk. Deborah walked briskly out the door. Well, so much for her rapport with the Rabbi. The honeymoon, apparently, was over.

"For God's sake, Deborah, you were supposed to help the congregation mend, not argue with the Rabbi and exacerbate the problems. Why did you get into a fight with him?" Barry Weinstein asked, agitated.

"I'm sorry, but if I'm in charge, then I'm in charge. I do what has to be done," Deborah was also angry.

"Come, come, now. We're all friends here. We can't be fighting like this. We're here to work things out together. I'll speak to Norman myself. He should be thrilled to sell that property. He'll make a fortune on it. I, myself, can think of at least three builders who would love to develop this property. It shouldn't make him sad, it should be music to his ears." Simmy Monash, who had obviously missed the point completely, said.

"That's a wonderful idea Simmy. Why don't you do that, and we can put the synagogue up for sale at the same time, because God knows there won't be anymore members," said Harry Levy, who, as usual, had accompanied Rochelle to the meeting. "I know I promised Rochelle that I would sit here quietly, as I usually do, and not say a word, but who could sit and listen to this crap? This is absurd."

Rochelle touched Harry's hand, a gesture meant to calm him down. She then stood up and raised her own voice. "I think the two of you have gone crazy. Deborah did the only thing there was to do. Any sensible person would realize that. Where does this Rabbi think he is, in Crown Heights with the Chasidim? It's time we began to stand up to him. This is our synagogue. We hired him, remember? He works for us."

"That's exactly right," Harry agreed, glancing at Rochelle before speaking. "This could never happen in business. In the real world he would be thrown out on his ass for overstepping his bounds. He is an employee and it's about time someone let him know that."

"The Synagogue is his boundary," Simmy shouted out, jumping up from his seat to make his point.

"Simmy, shut up and sit down," Harry said in a tone of voice Deborah had never heard him use before.

"Come, come now. Let's stop bickering among ourselves," Deborah said, banging a book on the table to get everyone's attention. "We've got to all work together here."

Chapter Eleven

September 1992

Deborah couldn't wait to get home to speak to Carl. He had always been her best audience. Even if she didn't like the suggestions he would make, just telling him a problem and watching his reaction would often help her to come up with a new idea herself. They were sitting on the couch in the den. Deborah had her feet propped up on an old wooden coffee table that visibly had seen the wear and tear of young children and a variety of pets.

"Can you believe any of this is really happening?" she sighed. "I don't know what to do. It's a crazy situation."

Carl listened intently. "Why don't you speak to Esther? I bet she'll have some thoughts on the subject."

"Speak to Esther? She's the Rabbi's wife. She couldn't say anything even if she wanted to."

"Don't be so sure. She's much more practical than the Rabbi is and she has to have some way to get him to listen to her. She couldn't possibly agree with what he's doing."

"I'm sure she doesn't, but she can't look like she's sabotaging him. She's the Rebbetzin, for God's sake."

Carl jumped up. "I almost forgot. Let's just relax for a few minutes and forget about all of this Temple stuff. I have a surprise for you."

Carl picked up an audio tape from the end table and handed it to her. "This came in the mail today," he smiled.

Their two sons, Brian and Seth, had both taken a year off from college to work on their music. They had recently formed a rock group and this was a copy of their first recording venture. They called themselves B.S. Rocks, and they were very excited about their new undertaking. As young adults, neither Deborah nor Carl would have been able to take time off to dedicate to themselves; the burden of their responsibilities had always loomed heavily on them. They were delighted that they could make it possible for their children to listen to their hearts and follow their own destiny.

When Brian was born, Deborah had wanted to name him Isaac, after her father. Carl had insisted that Isaac was not an American name and that it would prove to be an obstacle to him as he traveled through life. Deborah grudgingly agreed to give the baby the Hebrew name of *Yitzhak,* but in English, his very Americanized name was Brian.

When Brian and Seth were children Deborah had tried to instill in them her own love of music. The talent that her father and mother had bequeathed to her had been very evident to everyone as she was growing up. But Deborah never would have considered a career in music for herself. Being a musician could not provide a steady income for anyone, and Deborah needed to be practical. It was thrilling for her to realize that both her sons were also gifted musicians. She herself taught them to play the violin when they were very young, and by teaching them and listening to them play, she knew that somehow she was still in touch with her father. His essence lived on in the music her sons created, the part of his soul that even Treblinka had not been able to destroy.

As Brian and Seth got older they also studied piano, and Seth, younger and more gregarious than his older brother, even began to play the guitar. In high school both boys started to write original melodies and lyrics that they would practice in front of their parents and anyone else who would listen.

"I'm tone dead," Carl would tell them. "Bring it to your mother—she's the talented one."

They would perform at high school functions. Aunt Rose, Uncle Jacob, and Grandma Brina were their loudest cheering section. When they were seniors a group of freshman girls had even started a fan club for them.

Carl popped the tape into the stereo and they both leaned back, prepared to listen. "This is what's important, Deb," he told her. "This other stuff will eventually go away, but our boys are always here with us. They're ours. This is what really counts, now and forever."

"Forever can be just a moment in time," Deborah answered, again thinking of her father and wondering if it was possible for him to hear the music his grandchildren were creating. Was he with Rabbi Levinson? And if Rabbi Levinson was able to appear to her after he had died, why hadn't her own father ever come to visit?

November 15, 1992

The Executive Committee gathered at the Rabbi's home to give Esther some emotional support. Deborah arrived with Carl. Rochelle Levy was hanging tightly onto Harry's arm, as though she might fall if she let go. Every time she tried to speak she began to cry, so she remained silent, staring straight ahead into space. Harry Levy, generally an outgoing people-person, clearly was deeply affected by the Rabbi's death. He appeared to be heavily sedated. His eyes were glassy and his body movement was much like a robot. He didn't speak to anyone.

Simmy Monash greeted Deborah and Carl at the door.

"Can you believe such a thing could happen?" he asked, crying and blowing his nose into his large white handkerchief. "That such a man can be cut down in cold blood. This is getting to be worse than my country. Where should I be able to move to next?"

"I am so sorry," Deborah pushed past Simmy and embraced Esther. "Is there anything I can do for you?"

"No, I don't think so. Nothing seems very real at the moment. I'm not usually at a loss for what to say, but I'm feeling very overwhelmed. Between the police and the newspapers . . . I don't know, I can't even think." Esther pulled a tissue from a box on the end table and wiped her eyes. "The awful thing is that he would have wanted to be buried within twenty-four hours, you know how important that would be to him, with all his body parts intact," she quickly added. "But the police are insisting that they have to do an autopsy and if that wasn't bad enough, to add insult to injury, because of the autopsy we can't bury him for another two days. I just feel horrible. First some crazed lunatic comes along and kills him and now his simplest wishes regarding burial can't even be followed."

"I didn't realize they were doing an autopsy. Carl, did you know they were doing an autopsy?" Deborah turned to her husband.

"I believe in a case like this it's the law. They have to do an autopsy."

"Esther," Deborah asked, "have you spoken to Detective Brody? He's Jewish, you know. He understands our traditions. Maybe he can help speed things up."

Esther was still sobbing. "I have spoken to him. He's very sympathetic, but there's nothing anyone can do. They tell me that when someone is murdered, the rules are different."

Barry Weinstein jumped in. "At least it will give us time to notify the whole congregation and other rabbis in the area. I know everyone who can make it will want to come to the funeral. The turnout will be tremendous."

"My God, Barry," Deborah sighed, jabbing him with her elbow. "I don't think that's what Esther is concerned about at the moment. We can take care of those things without involving her. Leon will see to it that everyone in the congregation is called."

Deborah and Carl did not stay at the Levinson home very long. Deborah felt certain that what Esther Levinson really needed was some peace and quiet to sort out her own thoughts on what was happening, and she hoped that if she and Carl left, it would prompt others to follow suit, giving Esther some badly needed solitude. She wanted to tell Carl about her dream, which had been haunting her since Leon's initial phone call that morning, but Carl tended to be very concrete about these things. She knew he would never accept the idea of a dead Rabbi Levinson coming to her for what? Help? Maybe. She decided to wait until she could engender more emotional energy to discuss exactly what it all meant.

Deborah and Carl arrived home to find a phone message from Susan King. "I've been listening to the news all day and I can't believe what has happened. Call me as soon as you get in."

Deborah returned her call.

"I'm so glad you called back," Susan said upon hearing Deborah's voice. "Things must be really hectic for you right now."

"God, yes. I don't know how you do this for a living. I can't stand it."

"Well, I'm not usually emotionally involved with my clients. I can remain cool and keep some perspective on what's going on. You don't have that luxury right now."

"For sure. I can't stand much more of this, and the process is just getting started. It's bad enough dealing with Rabbi Levinson's death, but to try and imagine who murdered him? Well, I can't imagine who would want to kill the Rabbi."

"From what you've told me about him lots of people were not thrilled with some of his attitudes and tactics."

"That's true," Deborah responded, "but how do you leap from 'not thrilled with some of his attitudes' to murder? I can't think of anyone who would have murdered him. The people who didn't know him well still loved him and thought he was wonderful. After all, he performed all of their life-cycle events like Bar Mitzvahs and funerals. He married all of their children for God's sake. The more active congregants who knew him better may have been upset at his changing attitudes, but you know, these are reasonably religious people that are involved here and I can't imagine any of them shooting any rabbi, let alone their own rabbi."

Susan laughed. "Religious environments bring forth strong emotions. People who become emotionally overwrought can become obsessed and, in a moment of great passion, commit murder. These are crimes of passion. The Bible is filled with such events. Remember Cain and Abel?"

"I know, but I just find it hard to believe that one of the people I am working with at the synagogue would murder anyone, let alone a Rabbi, their own Rabbi."

"Is it possible that Rabbi Levinson was murdered by someone not connected to your synagogue?"

"It appears as though whoever killed him might have had a key to the synagogue building; that would almost have to make it a member, and worse than that, it would have to be a member who is active or had been active enough at one time to have been given a key."

"That's too bad. But think about your own life experience before you absolve all of your acquaintances. We are all human, and human beings under extreme pressure, for whatever reason, are capable of murder."

"I guess you're right," Deborah sighed. "It's just difficult to come up with a name or a motive that is strong enough."

"Maybe it will turn out that it was someone outside of your little 'in-group' after all. Rabbis touch a lot of lives on a daily basis, and I have had clients who were very creative about simple needs, like getting keys to a building. You'd be surprised how easy something like that can be if you're intent upon getting the job done."

"I suppose that's possible," Deborah answered, "but you'll have to excuse me. This has been an exhausting day, and I must go to sleep."

"Of course. I just wanted you to know that my office is at your disposal and we are very well equipped to deal with murder investigations. If I can be of service, don't hesitate to call."

"Thank you, and good night."

❧

Deborah canceled all of her appointments other than court appearances for the rest of the week. It wouldn't be fair to be charging clients for her time when she would never be able to concentrate on their problems. The following morning was Wednesday, Carl's usual day off. He did get up early to make some hospital visits, but he was home before 10:00. When he arrived, Deborah and Detective Brody were having coffee together in the kitchen.

"Good morning, Dr. Katzman. I'm glad you're here. I have some questions to ask you too."

Carl nodded. "I'm afraid I can't tell you much. The Rabbi was unconscious the whole time I worked on him."

"Well, I think it would be helpful if you could sit down and join us for a little while. I'll try to make it brief. Incidentally, there were no prints on the gun, which should rule out a suicide."

"A man as religious as Rabbi Levinson would never commit suicide," Deborah stated emphatically.

"I don't disagree with you, but we had to rule it out before we could move on. He was shot at very close range, under any circumstances," Detective Brody shook his head in disbelief.

"That's correct," Carl agreed. "Of course, Detective, Deb and I want to do everything we can to help you find the murderer. It's hard to believe that anyone could be callous enough to murder our Rabbi, no matter how upset they might have been with him."

"On the theory that the murderer let himself, or herself, into the building, maybe we can start by your giving me the names of all of the people who had keys to the basement door of the Temple." Detective Brody's tone had become more business-like.

Deborah smiled. "Do you belong to a Reform synagogue, Detective?" she asked.

"Now, how did you figure that out, Mrs. Katzman?"

Deborah hesitated. "I don't want you to be upset if I tell you."

"I promise, I will not be upset," Detective Brody grinned.

"Well, it's just that when you used the word 'Temple,' I had a flashback to one of Rabbi Levinson's many lectures. He once said it was only Reform synagogues that called themselves 'Temples' because they didn't know any better. He believed that a 'Temple' was a pagan house of worship, very different from a 'synagogue,' which was uniquely Jewish. But you have to understand that Rabbi Levinson had become extraordinarily unaccepting of differences in recent years," Deborah was quick to add.

Detective Brody laughed, he didn't seem to be the slightest bit disturbed. "Like I told you before, 'Two Jews, Three Shuls.' That's just the way it is. My wife insisted upon a Reform *shul* because she wanted my daughter to have the same training as my son. For me, anyplace where Jews come together is a good place to be, no matter what we call ourselves."

"Amen," Carl agreed, glaring at Deborah for bringing up the subject.

"I'm sorry I said anything at all," Deborah apologized. "It's just that as you spoke, I could actually hear his voice. I suppose that will happen a lot until my mind begins to really absorb the fact that he's not around anymore."

"That's fine, ma'am," Detective Brody responded in his most soothing manner. "I understand how upset you all are. But if we could just get back to the basement door of the synagogue, once again." He smiled, dragging out the word "synagogue" as he spoke.

Deborah laughed; she liked Detective Brody.

"Lots of people have keys, I think," she said. "The lock on the basement door matches the lock on the main entrance. Anybody who has the key to one door has the key to both doors."

"Can you give me a list of all of those people, then?"

"Well, I think Leon Feldman can give you a better idea than I can. I'm happy to tell you the people I know who have keys, but Leon, I'm sure, can add to that list." Deborah began to think about the matter at hand.

"Yes, and we are going to get to Mr. Feldman in a few minutes, but first, you tell me what you know, please, ma'am."

Carl reached in back of him and pulled a pad and pencil off the counter by the telephone. "Why don't you call out the names and I'll write them down, Deb?"

Carl was poised, ready to begin writing. Deborah knew that Carl had come home to help because he thought she needed him. That was their relationship, she was independent until she needed him, and then Carl would run to her side; he'd be there for her to lean on, a cushion to keep her from banging her head on the hard ground, like a husband or the caring father she had never known. Carl took good care of himself, and physically no one would have realized that he was nine years her senior, and despite all of her own accomplishments, over the years she had become quite accustomed to holding tightly on to his hand when life became difficult. Nevertheless, Deborah had yet to tell him about her dream. She knew that she had to speak to him about it very soon. Carl was always so practical, she knew what his reaction would be, but they were a team and she was obsessed with the vision of Rabbi Levinson hovering over her bed. Carl had to know.

Deborah suddenly realized Detective Brody was waiting for her to speak.

"Well," she began, "first, all of the officers, the Sisterhood President, Brotherhood President".

"Just one moment, please," interrupted Detective Brody. "Can you give me the names, along with the positions, and tell me something about the people involved?"

"Of course, I'm sorry." Deborah continued, "Rochelle Levy is the Sisterhood President. She's a wonderful woman, very devoted to the synagogue and very loyal. She's also very bright. She works as a part-time bookkeeper and has been the Temple Treasurer several times over the years. If she were twenty years younger, she probably would have become a CPA instead of a bookkeeper."

"Do you know if she owns a gun?" Detective Brody asked.

"I have no idea," answered Deborah.

"I'm positive she doesn't," Carl jumped in.

"Why are you so sure?" Deborah asked him.

"Because she is a 'lady,' a product of her generation, and she hates guns. I can't imagine her owning one," Carl persisted. "She is a patient of mine and I know her very well. Believe me, she doesn't own a gun, and is not capable of killing anyone, I'm quite sure."

Deborah turned toward Detective Brody and frowned. "I am a holocaust survivor, Detective. In my lifetime I have learned that people you would least expect to be violent are capable of committing extraordinary atrocities." This was a rare occasion. Deborah was usually careful not to mention her personal history to anyone outside of her own family, but somehow Detective Brody's friendly manner made him seem almost like family. "I am very fond of Rochelle and I can't imagine her murdering the Rabbi or anyone else, but I wouldn't knock her out on the basis of her being unable to shoot a gun, because under the right circumstances, I honestly believe that everyone is capable of shooting a gun."

Carl cleared his throat and squirmed uncomfortably in his chair, as he was prone to do whenever he feared Deborah might be alluding to those years in her life he would rather not deal with. He had become a very good listener during the time they had been married, always giving Deborah the support he knew she needed, but he had never been able to become comfortable with his wife's past, perhaps because she herself was still obsessed with her past. It was always there, the ghost that never faded into the walls around them. Their sons grew up understanding the difference between their house and their friends' houses. They lived as others did, rarely discussing the fact that they never knew their grandfather, that their mother still spoke with a British accent, that their grandmother, their Uncle Jacob and their Aunt Rose, on certain Jewish holidays or while looking at old photos, or talking about lost relatives, would begin to cry with seemingly no provocation, and that at certain times in their lives, individually and as a family, they suddenly would become despondent, and in those moments would need an extraordinary amount of support, both individually and collectively.

Detective Brody went on, determined to get the information he was seeking. "So tell me, is there someone around who you believe would be more likely to use a gun? Maybe that's the place to start."

As she spoke, Detective Brody's eyes were focused on her face. His eyes stared at her so intensely that Deborah felt he could see right through to her soul.

"Simmy Monash is from Iran. He might use a gun. He's a hard person to figure out."

"Absolutely," Carl agreed, "Simmy would definitely use a gun. Of course, I can't imagine him killing the Rabbi, not that I don't think he's capable of it. His whole manner is so strange. It's hard to know what he's capable of, but I say that only because he seems to feel phenomenal reverence for the position."

"What did he do in Iran?" Detective Brody asked.

"Carl and Deborah looked at each other and shrugged. "Who knows?" said Deborah. "Whatever he did though, he must have made a lot of money doing it, because he and his family live very well, and I can't imagine that he has earned that kind of money renting condos in Mineola, which is the business he says he's in at the moment."

"I wouldn't be too sure. People can make a lot of money in real estate, ma'am," Detective Brody answered. "Although if he's from Iran he has to be tough. He couldn't have gotten out otherwise."

"Hotels, houses, that's money-making business," Deborah replied. "But just renting apartments on two-year leases? I don't think so."

"Well, let's go on with some other names."

"Barry Weinstein," Deborah continued, "and it's also hard for me to think of him as a murderer, much less someone who would murder the Rabbi."

"Tell me about him," the Detective probed.

"Well, he's got his own clothing manufacturing firm. I think he's importing men's clothing from China or some other third-world country. I know he travels a lot on business. He seems to make good money. He's got a nice house and his children are in private school. He's very devoted to Beth Torah. He was supposed to be President this year, but because of all the infighting, I was asked to come in as a sort of babysitter to try and calm things down a bit. At this point, that certainly seems a bit ludicrous, doesn't it?"

"And this will probably end up being your fault too," Carl said, smiling. "You were right. I certainly called this wrong. You never should have accepted this job in the first place."

Deborah explained for the benefit of Detective Brody. "When they asked me to run for President, I didn't want to do it. Carl thought I would enjoy it. It seemed like a good idea to him."

"I've learned that there is more to a Jewish education than what I learned in Hebrew school," Carl chuckled.

"Anyone else?" asked Detective Brody.

"There were lots of people who were angry, but I don't know who else had keys to the building."

"Please don't take offense, but I just have to ask this question," Detective Brody sounded somewhat embarrassed, "Where were you at 7:30 this morning?"

"She was sleeping," Carl responded before Deborah could reply. "I left the house at 7:00 and Deb was still snoring."

"Excuse me," Deborah asked, almost in a whisper, "but exactly what time did Rabbi Levinson die?"

"I think it was about a quarter to 9:00," Carl responded.

Deborah suddenly felt a heaviness that was hard to describe. It was as if the room was closing in on her. She coughed to keep herself from choking. Eight-forty-five was the time the Rabbi came to see her. Once again she envisioned Rabbi Levinson hovering over her bed, trying to tell her . . . what, exactly? Could the Rabbi be in the room with them at this very moment, as they were speaking? Was the heaviness she felt actually the presence of Rabbi Levinson? Or was it merely the overactive imagination of a holocaust survivor? How could she ever discuss this with Carl? How could she ever discuss this with anyone?

"Who's the group starting the new Temple, I mean, *shul*," Detective Brody asked, seeming not to notice Deborah's abrupt mood change.

Deborah took a deep breath. "Temple is fine, really," she answered. "I guess I'll never live this down."

"I'm just joking a bit at your expense," he said with a grin, waiting for an answer.

Deborah's mood remained somber. "The members of the Young Couples Club and their friends, I believe, are the most active members looking for radical change. They were threatening to leave. They want more recognition for women. I think that's their main issue. You know, a Bat Mitzvah for their daughters on Saturday morning instead of Friday night; they want to be counted in the *minyan*—all of the things your wife joined a Reform temple to get, although none of those people have keys to the building that I'm aware of. You'd have to speak to Leon to find out about that, though."

"I'm going to see him as soon as I leave here," Detective Brody replied.

"And before I forget," Deborah suddenly remembered, "we've had a bit of a fiasco involving Norman Gross and his son-in-law, Fred Kaplan, over the property they own off Main Street, across from Beth Torah."

"You mean Norman Gross from Gross Development Corp?" Detective Brody asked.

"That's the family," Deborah answered. "The Rabbi made some new friends who live in the retirement facility in town. They began coming to our *minyan* and they objected to Norman allowing our congregants to park on his property on *Shabbos*. The Rabbi agreed with them, and actually that was the fight that we were in the middle of when he was killed."

"It's hard to believe that the *great* Rabbi Levinson was having these kinds of problems within his own congregation. No one in the larger Jewish community would believe it."

Deborah smiled. "Until I became President, I didn't believe it either. I had no idea of how unreasonable he could be. I presume that over the years his charisma got him through a lot of tough places, but he was at a point where it was no longer going to work and he was becoming less and less charismatic and more and more arrogant."

"One last thing before I leave," Detective Brody interrupted. "What can you tell me about the Rebbetzin? I know that she's a social worker and that she works for CARE in the city, but I want to know what she's like."

"Esther?" Deborah asked, with some surprise. "She's a strong, independent woman. Very different from the kind of person you'd think Rabbi Levinson would be married to. They each appeared to be very supportive, very devoted. For important issues they seemed to be there for each other, but she's a hard woman to understand; sometimes she can be very aloof, but that may just be a facade she's had to develop to allow her to continue working with the underprivileged. If you don't begin to build a shell around yourself, I imagine it can become an impossible job to stay with for any length of time.

"The Rabbi's mother actually acted as the more 'traditional Rebbetzin' for him. Esther and his mother each seemed to know their roles; there didn't appear to be any overlapping of responsibility or any disagreement about it, and it's worked quite well for them over the years."

"I agree, our Rebbetzin can be one tough cookie," Carl added, "but they were a very devoted couple, and from her reaction at the hospital she is completely devastated by his death. After all, they have no children so they just had each other. I can't imagine what she is going to do without him."

Detective Brody stood up. "It's unusual for a Rabbi not to have children, particularly a Rabbi as traditional as you tell me this man was. Do you know why they never had children?"

Deborah began to answer, "Rumor has it that Esther was too career minded."

"Is that what you think?" he asked.

"No. Actually, I'd be willing to bet that for whatever reason, she just never conceived. I think it would be very unusual for a woman of Esther's generation to make a conscious decision not to have children, particularly given their position in the Jewish community, but since they never spoke about it, no one really knows for sure," Deborah replied.

Carl nodded in agreement. "I can't think of any patients in their age group who actually chose not to have children. They either had them or adopted them. Once in a rare while you meet people who just couldn't conceive or had genetic diseases that were yet untreatable and for whatever reason they didn't want to adopt, but it's not that common. And couples as traditional as Esther and Rabbi Levinson, I can't imagine them deciding not to have children."

"Thank you. Well, I have to move on," said Detective Brody, heading towards the front door. "You have both certainly given me enough to begin working on. I will stop by and see Mr. Feldman at the synagogue. It would be good if we could touch base with each other often, just so I can keep on top of things. You'll be hearing from me very soon. The murder of a popular Rabbi has created quite a stir. The newspapers won't leave us alone until we arrest someone. Hopefully it will be the right someone. From the top of the department on down there's a lot of pressure being put on us. We've really got to get this thing solved quickly.

"If I don't get in touch with you and you have some news, be sure to call me. Actually I'd like to speak with you a few times a week for the time being, Mrs. Katzman. I need your help."

"Whatever you say, and please call me Deborah."

The door had not yet closed completely behind Detective Brody when Carl spun around to face Deborah. He put his hand on her shoulder and asked, "What's wrong?"

"What do you mean?"

"I know something happened to you while you were speaking to Detective Brody. It was as if you were in a trance, off in another world."

"If I tell you what I am dealing with, you're not going to believe me."

"Why would I not believe you? Of course, I'll believe you."

"You have to promise me that you will take what I say very seriously."

"Since when don't I take everything you say very seriously? Come on, Deb, stop it."

"Okay, I'll tell you, but be very careful about what you do with what I'm about to say.

"It's odd that you should use the expression that I appeared to be 'in another world,' because at 8:45 on the morning of his death, Rabbi Levinson came to speak to me."

"You don't really believe that?" Carl appeared startled.

"Listen to me, it's true. I have not lost my mind. I was dreaming about him. He was trying to tell me something, but I couldn't hear him. When I awoke he was hovering above me at the end of the bed. I'm telling you, I saw him."

"And what do you think it is that he was trying to tell you?"

"Maybe he was trying to tell me who killed him," she whispered.

"Deb, get real. You had a dream, that's all. It was nothing more than that. People have dreams all the time."

"I never had a dream about Rabbi Levinson before, and you don't think it's strange that I had a dream about him at the very moment of his death?"

"I don't know, but I wouldn't be talking about this too much to other people, not everyone knows you as well as I do."

"You don't believe me. See, that's why I didn't want to tell you."

"I do believe you. I believe you had the dream, but that's all it was: a dream. You surely don't think Rabbi Levinson came back from the dead to ask you for help, do you? He wasn't even speaking to you when he died, why would he come to you? If he was going to appear to anyone, it would have been to Esther."

"I don't know why he came to me. There's a Kabbalistic belief that the spirit, upon dying, roams through the world until its deeds have been requited. Maybe Rabbi Levinson came to me because he wanted to make peace before moving on."

"I think you ought to put this out of your mind. It doesn't mean anything, believe me. Patients of mine have dreams all the time. Rabbi Levinson was causing you all kinds of grief, it's not unusual that you would have had a dream about him."

"I don't know what to believe, but I do know what I saw."

"Okay," Carl responded. "Let's say Rabbi Levinson came to speak to you or to make peace with you, or whatever. So? What happens next?"

"I think it's up to me to find his murderer."

"If that's how you're interpreting this dream, that's fine. There's nothing wrong with our working with the police to find his murderer."

"But you don't believe I saw what I saw."

"I believe in you and in your ability to do what you set out to do, and that should be enough for both of us."

Deborah sighed. She knew that as far as Carl was concerned, this was the most she could hope for.

Chapter Twelve

November 22, 1992

T he Long Island newspaper headlines read: "Funeral for Murdered Rabbi to Take Place at Synagogue Beth Torah. Thousands Expected to Attend."

The funeral was larger than any event *The* Synagogue had ever imagined would take place in their Sanctuary. The Yom Kippur crowd could only pale by comparison. There were representatives from UJA/Federation, Jewish Theological Seminary, every Zionist organization in the City, and Rabbis from all the neighboring congregations. Every group the Rabbi had ever connected with at any time in his life was visibly present. People were standing in the street in front of the building, and Leon had to have speakers set up outside the synagogue itself to allow those latecomers who couldn't fit into the sanctuary to hear what was being said.

Rochelle Levy sat in the front pew; to her right were the Sisterhood officers, all weeping quietly and leaning on each other for support; to her left was her husband, Harry. Harry had his arm around Rochelle's shoulders, trying to comfort her, but he appeared to be deep into his own thoughts. He had a glazed look in his eyes as though he were in a distant place, far away from what was going on around him.

Simmy Monash and Barry Weinstein stood in the back of the Synagogue greeting everyone and helping to seat congregants as they arrived. With each new group that came through the massive black doors, Simmy would begin to cry and moan into his now-familiar, large, white handkerchief. Barry would grab hold of each person's hand, while shaking his head in somber disbelief.

"Terrible, terrible," said Leon Feldman to everyone he passed. "What a world this is!"

Esther entered the sanctuary with Rabbi Cohen, a former classmate of the dearly departed who happened to be the new President of the New York Board of Rabbis and the Rabbi whom she had chosen to eulogize her husband. They were accompanied by Deborah and Carl, who escorted Rabbi Levinson's father to his seat. Sonia Levinson appeared pale and waif-like, but as attractive as ever. Her husband held on to her arm and stared straight ahead. They clearly were leaning on each other for strength.

Carl was attempting to speak to Dr. Levinson regarding the medical trauma that caused his son's death, but wasn't sure that Dr. Levinson heard anything he said.

Deborah held on tightly to Sonia Levinson's quivering hand.

As each person stopped in front of them to verbalize their sympathy, the expression on Esther's face grew more and more strained, but she said little. Sonia wept openly. Her tears washed away the makeup that hid the surgeon's two thin, faint scars in front of her ears.

"No mother should live long enough to bury her child," she sobbed. "And what a wonderful son he was!"

Deborah squeezed her hand. She, too, was a mother.

"Excuse me for one moment, please," Esther mumbled to Deborah and Carl in a solemn tone, "I have to talk to Saul by myself, I have to explain to him why I couldn't bury him within twenty-four hours. I want to make sure he understands."

"Of course," Deborah and Carl both nodded sympathetically. Deborah wondered if Rabbi Levinson might also have visited Esther immediately after his passing.

Esther walked toward the closed coffin. In keeping with Jewish custom and her husband's wishes, the coffin was a plain, pine box. Unfortunately, being preoccupied by other matters, Esther hadn't noticed the four small slanted legs attached to each corner of the coffin's base that jut out ever so slightly into the aisle. Esther stared into space, not focusing on anyone, realizing that all eyes were on her. She attempted to concentrate on the task at hand, to come up with just the right words for this difficult moment, but as she approached Saul, she inadvertently stepped onto one of the slanted wooden legs that were protruding into her path, lost her footing and fell, face-forward over the coffin. She lay there very still, burying her face in her hands to hide her embarrassment.

The headline in *Newsday* read: "Rabbi's Wife Faints Over Coffin While Congregation Weeps."

Chapter Thirteen

December 1992

Deborah continued to give as much information as she could to the local newspapers, hoping they would stop asking questions about who she believed the murderer was.

The board of directors held an emergency meeting and voted to give a six-month contract to Rabbi Klein, a recently retired Rabbi from a large congregation in Westchester.

Deborah was attempting to catch up with the work load she had been neglecting and trying to get back into her normal routine when she received a phone call from Joey Miller, a charismatic young colleague she knew from committee lunches at the Bar Association. He was a real estate lawyer primarily and clearly had friends or family with money because he was buying up property all over Manhattan and Brooklyn. Circumstances had caused Deborah to fall behind in her schedule but she still had clients who were paying her well and she knew that she had an obligation to get back to work. Joey spoke to her about handling a situation for his parents. Deborah was not anxious to bring a new case into the office at this point in time, but Joey had a way about him and she didn't want to say no, so she promised him that she would speak to his father, Oscar, whenever he called, and decide if she would be able to help him.

"Sorry about your Rabbi," Joey said to her before saying goodbye.

"Thanks. It's been a difficult time," Doborah answered.

"You know, I had gone to visit him about six months ago."

"Really, for what?"

"Well, I was thinking of joining your synagogue. But I've been in this relationship with a woman for a few years. She's Asian and a Buddhist, and in my conversation with Rabbi Levinson it became clear that he would never marry a Jew to a non-Jew. I told him we would raise our kids as Jews, but he was adamant about diluting the race or some such crap, so I joined the Reconstructionist synagogue instead."

"So did you get married?"

"Still thinking about it."

"I've been critical of Rabbi Levinson for many reasons, but really I think any Conservative Rabbi would have felt similarly."

"Well, times are changing and these Rabbis have to change with the times. All over the world Jews look like the population they're living with. That's because they got together with their neighbors and made some babies. It's ridiculous for us to be so insular. And Rabbi Levinson had told me that even if he did marry us, our children wouldn't be considered Jewish no matter how we raised them because in order to be Jewish, the mother has to be Jewish. How absurd is that? You think our genes know which side of the family they came from?"

Deborah was weary and knew this was not the right moment for her to have this conversation. Like any good lawyer, she could make a case for either side, but she already had enough on her plate for the time being.

"I'll get back to you soon. Thanks for thinking of me," she said.

It was time to get back to work.

Joey's parents, Monica and Oscar Miller, were newly retired. They had a strong marriage and thought that retirement would offer them time to enjoy life. Oscar had been a Wall Street success story and Monica particularly enjoyed the luxurious lifestyle that his success in business brought them. She was smart and attractive and could be counted on to charm the affluent men and women they came into contact with. Oscar took pride in Monica's appearance, and loved her for the respect she commanded within the intellectual community they were part of. He knew that he was sharp enough and abrasive enough to earn the big bucks Wall Street had to offer, but without Monica to guide him, he would not have been included in the sophisticated New York art scene.

Until recently Monica and Oscar had for many years lived in a penthouse apartment on Fifth Avenue in Manhattan, overlooking the Central Park Zoo. When their son Joey was a little boy Monica would bring him to the zoo several times a week and she was certain that they both had a special relationship with many of the animals that resided there. She was convinced the monkeys recognized them and gave them a special greeting each time they visited. However, Joey was now a grown man, a successful real estate attorney. Oscar and Monica were proud of him, but Monica sorely missed the early years when she and Joey would spend hours strolling through the zoo together.

"One day Joey will get married and you'll have grandchildren to bring to the zoo," Oscar would tell her, but Joey was thirty-four, working at least forty-five to fifty hours a week, and while he had been involved with a pleasant young woman for a number of years, he appeared not to be very interested in marrying anyone.

Monica was an amateur artist. One of the rooms in their Fifth Avenue apartment was set up as her studio where she would often enjoy putting some of her ideas onto a fresh canvass. Together with Oscar she was a patron of the arts, hosting many events at the Museum of Modern Art as well as their favorite art galleries in Soho.

Time passed by and Oscar retired. Monica had severe knee problems that made traversing the streets of New York more and more difficult. She was too proud to appear at social events with a walker and began to avoid those occasions. Life in Manhattan had lost its appeal. From speaking to other women she learned that knee surgery was painful and she didn't want to go through that ordeal. At Oscar's suggestion they sold their apartment and purchased a luxurious home in East Hampton. The house overlooked the bay and before moving Monica envisioned herself sitting on the beach, perhaps taking art lessons from a local artist and creating wonderful seascapes and landscapes of the magnificent surroundings. This would be a new chapter in their lives, a quieter chapter, probably the final chapter, and she was excited to start anew. Unfortunately, moving to East Hampton proved to be very disappointing.

Oh, the new house was certainly plush and very impressive and Monica loved working with a decorator to make it comfortable for them to live in, even if it did appear to be a bit pretentious. The view, of course, remained magnificent; however, Monica was surprised to discover that the beach club located a little more than a block from their house brought an enormous amount of traffic into the area. It had seemed to both she and Oscar that the club was located far enough away that it wouldn't be an issue, but that proved not to be the case. When sitting outdoors on the front lawn during the summer months, Monica was subjected to both the noise of the traffic and the odor of the gas fumes and that made it impossible to enjoy painting. In addition, the beach attracted more people than she had anticipated and whenever Monica would attempt to paint on the beach, a crowd would form around her to see what she was doing, and it would become difficult for her to work. Monica had found the move from Manhattan to Long Island to be extremely exhausting and although she was not looking forward to moving again, she had begun to look at the real estate ads in other parts of the Hamptons.

Oscar spent his mornings reading the newspaper. He often played golf with former Wall Street colleagues now living nearby, and each day he would go online to check their stocks and rearrange his own investments, which at this point in time had become somewhat conservative in nature—although Oscar was still known to take a chance on something a bit risky when his experience and instincts convinced him it was a chance worth taking. Oscar's risk-taking concerned Monica and so they decided to maintain individual investment accounts rather than joint accounts. Monica preferred keeping her share of their money in treasury bonds and blue-chip stocks. Oscar was content generally, but often bored.

One morning, upon reading the newspaper, Oscar rushed into the bedroom where Monica was still sleeping to inform her that the beach club she found so distracting had declared bankruptcy.

"This is great," Oscar said enthusiastically. "We can buy the club out of bankruptcy and shut it down. I am going to call Joey and see if he knows a bankruptcy lawyer we can work with."

Joey was very skeptical of his father's plan, but he recommended Deborah Katzman as the bankruptcy lawyer he thought Oscar should contact. "Deb's got her head screwed on straight," he had said, "and she always uses good judgment in dealing with her clients. Listen to whatever she tells you because she is someone you can trust."

Monica was ecstatic at the possibility of getting rid of the beach club. "That would be fabulous," she told Oscar, "We can just hold on to the property and knock down the buildings. Joey can do what he wants with the property after we're gone." This was one risky investment she was happy to be part of. This was something she would be delighted to invest in herself.

That same day, Oscar contacted Deborah Katzman.

"So you want me to go into court, negotiate with the creditors and make certain that you buy this beach club out from under the current owners. Am I understanding you correctly?" Deborah asked.

"Exactly," said Oscar. "Make your best deal, but I want to do this regardless of the cost."

"Why do you want to own a beach club?" Deborah asked.

"I don't want to own a beach club. I want to knock the club down and have some peace and quiet in the neighborhood," Oscar replied.

"Well, this is sort of an unusual request. It's not unusual to buy someone out of bankruptcy, but destroying a popular beach club is certain to cause some excitement. I will call and find out when the case is on the calendar and I will contact the trustee and the creditors," Deborah explained. "I will have my paralegal get to work on that and I'll get back to you."

Deborah arrived at Bankruptcy Court for the Eastern District of New York, which was located in the Town of Hauppauge in Suffolk County. Brothers Bob and Kevin Richmond were the current owners of the club. They had been negotiating with their creditors and had declared bankruptcy in an effort to dispose of the debt they incurred while overspending on a new French restaurant they recently had constructed on the site. They had overspent on a very lavish French décor to ensure that the restaurant appeared authentic. Deborah had contacted Leonard Katz, the U.S. Trustee on the case, in advance to let him know that she had a client who was prepared to give the beach club creditors a better deal than they had negotiated with the current owners.

"How much money is your client prepared to spend?" the Trustee had asked.

"As much as it takes," she had answered.

Given the unexpected nature of Deborah's phone call, Len Katz had taken it upon himself to notify the Mayor of the Town of East Hampton that Deborah was planning to attend the next meeting on the case, which was actually scheduled for the following day. In addition to the taxes the beach club paid to the town, the club also attracted a good deal of business into the area and the Mayor, being somewhat concerned over this sudden turn of events, decided to send Neil Sherman, the town lawyer to the meeting as his representative, to make sure that nothing was going to happen that could destroy the working relationship that currently existed between the Town of East Hampton and the East Hampton Beach Club, regardless of who the owner was.

Leonard Katz, anxious to find out exactly what it was that Deborah had to say, began the meeting right on time. Deborah had intentionally arrived early as she was hoping to have an opportunity to speak to several of the creditors in advance of the meeting. The few creditors she did have an opportunity to speak to were very receptive to what she had to say and were prepared to now reject the plan that was on the table and begin to negotiate anew with Deborah on behalf of Monica and Oscar Miller.

"Do your clients have experience with running a beach club?" the Trustee inquired.

"No, they don't, but it doesn't matter because they have no intention of running the property as a beach club," Deborah replied.

"What are they planning to do with the property?" asked Rusty Gallo, the attorney representing the Richmond brothers. The brothers were obviously both more than a little surprised and visibly distressed.

"Their plan is to demolish the buildings and to leave the property vacant in order to put an end to the crowding and the level of noise that the club brings to the community."

Neil Sherman was attempting to exude a calm exterior, but Deborah had noticed the occasional twitching of his left eye and she quickly realized that he was anything but calm. She wondered if anyone else around the table had picked up on that. Neil Sherman addressed himself both to the trustee and to Rusty Gallo. "That would be quite detrimental to the Town of East Hampton. The beach club brings a good deal of business to the retail establishments in the town, and it would, additionally, cause the town to lose tax revenue. I think that the trustee should reject this offer and continue with the plan we were previously negotiating with the current owners of the beach club."

The club owners perked up.

"Your obligation is to the creditors, not to the town," Deborah interrupted. We are clearly prepared to give the creditors a much more lucrative package. They're already losing a good deal of money and it's unfair to expect them to take on a larger burden than they need to unnecessarily."

The creditors all nodded in agreement.

"Can we have another adjournment so I can speak to the Mayor about this?" Neil Sherman asked.

"Well, this is an unusual turn of events," Len Katz replied. "This shouldn't really involve the Mayor. I do agree that our obligation is to the creditors, but I will give everyone a few days to see if the parties can speak to each other and find a solution to the situation that will be satisfactory to everyone involved."

—❧—

Deborah decided to contact Joey Miller before calling his parents.

"This is going to be somewhat of a problem," Deborah explained. "The town is clearly upset at the thought of losing both tax revenue and business for the local retailers. I'm not sure how rational your father's thinking is about this."

Joey laughed. "My father is always rational, and he's accustomed to getting what he wants. He didn't earn all of his money by accepting what people told him. On Wall Street he was a real bull, someone who was always ahead of the pack—a knowledgeable risk-taker. He does his homework and he usually knows what he is doing. I don't invest a penny of my own money without speaking to him first."

"Okay, but I don't know if he's ever taken on a town before."

"Well, perhaps you'll be able to work out a plan of some sort with the town and the current owners that my father will be willing to go along with."

"My miracle basket seems to be empty at the moment. Your father seems quite adamant about what he wants."

"Just to give you a heads up," Joey said, "my mom is actually the instigator here. I doubt that my father even noticed the noise until she brought it to his attention, but he will do anything to make her happy. My dad is a bit hard of hearing and I'm sure that the noise is not bothering him in the least. My mother is the one who has to be appeased, and while she appears to be sweet and mellow, she can throw some pretty good punches when she deems it necessary. She retired to East Hampton in order to focus on her artistic endeavors, and the noise and the traffic from that beach club are preventing her from doing that. Send the traffic away from their street and you probably have a plan that will work."

"Thanks. Perhaps that's an idea we can work with."

Neil Sherman called Deborah's office the following morning. "We only have a few days to try to work things out before meeting with the trustee again, so perhaps you and I should try to get together as soon as possible."

"Of course," Deborah replied. "However, my time is very limited at this point. In addition to having a court appearance in Southern District tomorrow, I have a personal issue that's keeping me quite busy."

"Does that have to do with your Rabbi?" Neil Sherman inquired. "I've been following the case in the newspaper. That's a real tragedy. Rabbi Levinson was probably among the most respected Rabbis on Long Island."

"Yes, he was," she answered, "but if you've been following the case, then you know how involved I am with it—in addition to my law practice which keeps me busy enough."

"Yes, I do know that you're president of the synagogue. How about tomorrow? Do you have any free time tomorrow?"

Deborah pulled out her calendar. "I can do 8:00 in the morning, but I only have an hour and a half."

"That's earlier than I normally start, but I'll do it. Where do you want to meet?" he asked.

"My office. As soon as we're done, I have to leave for Manhattan."

"Fair enough. I'll bring the donuts," he quipped.

"Only if you want to eat them. I love donuts, but they sure as hell don't love me and I don't want to start the day with a sugar frenzy. But just to give you something to think about, instead of donuts, you might want to arrive at my office with an idea that will change the traffic pattern of the beach club, because that's the only solution that might be acceptable to my client—and I'm saying 'might' because I'm not certain that anything will dissuade him."

The suggestion was unexpected and Neil was delighted to see that Deborah might have some flexibility. "I will have to speak to the Mayor about that, and I will call Rusty Gallo to see if he wants to join our meeting."

"Whatever you have to do."

Since they had so little time to work with, Deborah didn't see any reason to hold back on the only possibility of an idea she could put forward. She understood the frustration of the owners of the club and she certainly understood the Mayor's concerns, but she represented Oscar and Monica Miller, and her obligation was to them. However, if they could come up with a solution that would satisfy all of the parties involved, that was certainly something to strive for.

❧

Neil Sherman arrived at Deborah's office five minutes late. "Crazy traffic," he apologized. Rusty can't make the meeting, he has to be in court, but I'll fill him in later."

"That's fine, but I only have the time that I have. At nine-thirty I am leaving for the city and this meeting will be over."

"Well, then, enough pleasantries, let's get down to *tachlis*."

"*Tachlis*?" she asked, "How do you know what *tachlis* is?"

"My family's sir name used to be Schumacher. My grandfather changed it a lot of years ago."

Deborah laughed, "Well, I never would have taken you for being Jewish, but that won't help us resolve this problem, so let's move on."

Neil took a deep breath and started speaking. "The Mayor and I spent a lot of time on this yesterday afternoon. There is a possibility that we can build a new entrance and exit at the other end of the beach club; that would allow traffic to enter and exit from Montauk Highway, and we could close up the current entrance into the club. That would bring the flow of traffic right on to an area that is built for and accustomed to heavy traffic."

"Are you willing to put that plan in writing?" she asked.

"Well, as you know, the town can't move that quickly. We need permission from the Zoning Board and they won't be meeting for another week; a traffic light would have to be added as well at the new entrance. Then we have to get an architect to draw the plans and after that we will go look for a contractor to build whatever it is that we'll be building. We might even have to put out an RFP—you know how these things work as well as I do. Also, the club is private property and I can't be certain that the board will agree to spend town money to create an exit and entrance ramp to a private beach club."

"My clients are not walking away from this issue on a maybe. Put something that is clear-cut in writing and I'll bring it to them, but unless you can present something definitive, they're buying the club and shutting it down."

Neil Sherman was not surprised at Deborah's reply. He expected it. "Let's see if we can meet with Rusty and his clients," he continued. Maybe they'll have an idea we can work on together. I'll speak to them today. Can we meet this evening or tomorrow sometime?"

"Sure," Deborah replied, "tomorrow, same time, same place. My calendar is booked for the next three weeks at least. I'm starting an hour earlier than I usually do in order to be able to accommodate you, but that's the best I can do."

"I'll speak to Rusty and I will contact you later," he responded.

Deborah looked up from her calendar. "If 8:00 tomorrow morning is agreeable, just send me an e-mail to let me know. I'm busy all day today and you probably won't be able to reach me by phone."

Neil Sherman called the Mayor and immediately thereafter placed a call to Rusty Gallo who conferenced in the club owners. Neil repeated what Deborah had suggested and proposed the possibility of changing the path of traffic in and out of the club.

"Isn't there any member of the club who would consider lending you money to build a new entrance on to Montauk Highway?" he asked them.

"If someone were willing to lend us money do you think we would have declared bankruptcy? That's not even a possibility," said Kevin Richmond.

His brother Bob interjected, "Actually though, being able to access the club from the highway would definitely give us better exposure which possibly could bring in more members."

"Keep that thought," Rusty Gallo interjected. "If you allowed outsiders into the restaurant, perhaps charging a higher price than you do for members, and then put a flashing sign inside your gate that is visible from the highway, that would also bring in more restaurant business."

Rusty was spilling out ideas as they came to mind and his clients were listening carefully, trying to digest everything that was being said.

"You guys talk it over among yourselves and see if you can come up with a plan I can present to Deborah Katzman in the morning. Deborah is someone you should be able to deal with. She's logical and reasonable, but of course I don't know anything about her clients. They obviously have money and it's clear that they don't like your club. Call me before six o'clock this evening."

"We'll call you a lot sooner than that. I'm meeting my wife at five-thirty," Bob answered him.

Deborah once again arrived at her office bright and early the following morning. She had spoken to Oscar and he seemed somewhat open to the idea of changing the traffic pattern of the club, but only if the Mayor put it in writing. Deborah agreed that without ironclad assurances from the town, there was no way to be certain that anything would change.

Neil Sherman arrived at her office right on time carrying coffee in one hand and his briefcase in the other. Rusty Gallo arrived a few minutes later. The three of them walked into her conference room together.

"My assistant should be in any minute and then we can close the door and get to work," Deborah told them, but as soon as she finished speaking, Nancy walked through the door. "Good morning, Nancy. No interruptions, please, until our meeting is over."

"Of course," she replied, with a polite smile.

Neil Sherman began speaking immediately.

"I am going to present to the Mayor the possibility that the town pay for a new approach in and out of the beach club, and allow the club owners to continue negotiating their plan with the creditors. However, there is no guarantee that the Zoning Board will agree that the town should pay for that. I can tell you, frankly, that there is a good chance that the board will go for it as the club brings a lot of money into the town and they would not like to see that business go away. However, even if the Mayor called an emergency meeting, it would take at least a month, maybe more, to do what has to be done on the town level, and that's probably an optimistic estimate of the time involved. This is an improvement to private property that we're trying to get the town to pay for."

Rusty interjected, "The judge may not agree to another recess as the creditors are putting a lot of pressure on him and he is really *pissed* at my clients, if you will excuse my language, for having thrown so much money into what he is calling a "pie-in-the-sky" scheme with that restaurant they had built. That was what caused their money problems. They made an assumption that people would be willing to spend forty-five to fifty dollars a person for lunch and God knows how much for dinner. It just didn't work out, but by the time they realized that they had miscalculated they had already spent a fortune building the damn thing. And to make it worse, they tell me that they have a contract with some French chef that they are having difficulty getting out of. They can fire him, but according to the contract, if the restaurant remains open, they would be obligated to pay him at least one year's salary in advance regardless of whether he is working for them or not. If they don't fire him, they have a three-year contract with this chef that they're responsible for.

"The judge thinks these guys have behaved irresponsibly and I just don't think he will be sympathetic to a plan that's going to take another two months to begin to implement, especially when we're not even sure that it will pass through at the town level."

Neil Sherman nodded.

Deborah smiled. "I can bring any ideas you come up with to my clients, but they are not going to go away unless you can guarantee them that those cars will not be driving by their house to get to the beach club."

Rusty went on. "The irony of this is that if they actually do change the approach to the club so that you can enter and exit the premises from Montauk Highway, and if they then open the club restaurant to the public, chances are that the restaurant business will begin to boom and they then will be able to show a profit."

"So, then," Deborah replied, "the club should be able to find an investor to help them out."

Neil Sherman added, "There doesn't seem to be anyone on the scene. Maybe your client would like to invest some money in the club instead of tearing it down. Is that a possibility?"

"I don't know how much Oscar is willing to invest, but I can certainly bring that idea to him."

"Why don't you do that and we can all talk again at the end of the day?" Neil suggested.

Deborah called Oscar and Monica Miller as soon as the meeting ended. Oscar answered the phone.

"So let me get this straight," he said, upon hearing what Deborah had to say, "They expect me to pay for the noise I am trying to get rid of? Monica, come here, you won't believe this."

"Well, it's an investment," Deborah replied. "Joey tells me that you are still a serious investor. I thought that the idea of making money on a business that's right in your own neighborhood might appeal to you. You can walk over every day to see how they're doing. You could probably invest no more money than it would cost to knock the place down and have all the debris carted away, and we could make a deal that ensures that traffic would be diverted to Montauk Highway instead of the street you live on. You actually would be building something that makes the members of the club happy, rather than destroying an enterprise and causing many people to lose their jobs."

"The only person I care about being happy is my wife. Monica, what do you think?"

"I don't know about the business end of it," Monica responded. "I don't care if the club is there or if it's not there. I only care about getting rid of the noise and the smell of the cars constantly passing by."

Oscar saw the possibility of a deal in the making that could be very advantageous to his own cause. It could be a money-maker and he'd have something concrete to occupy his time. "Okay, I will tell you what I'm willing to do: I will pay off their creditors and I can take care of the renovations regarding the access in and out of the club from Montauk Highway, but in return I want seventy-five percent ownership of the club. The current owners can keep twenty-five percent and they can be the managers, but the final say on what happens at the club stays with me."

Deborah was surprised. Oscar Miller might be approaching 70, but his mind was still sharp as a tack. "Seventy-five/twenty-five is a bit much to ask them to swallow, don't you think, Oscar?"

Oscar smiled, "Well, you present that to them and see what they come back with. I don't like to deal with people who make bad decisions. These guys had grandiose ideas but they never made sure that they had enough capital to back it up. I could never trust them as partners. I need control or there is no deal. Go talk to them and let me know what they say."

"Twenty-five percent is out of the question," Rusty Gallo responded after hearing Oscar Miller's offer. "That's not a deal, that's annihilation."

Neil Sherman was also conferenced on the call. "I think you ought to present it to your clients and see what they have to say about it."

"Well, of course I have to present it to them, but I can't imagine they would go for such an unfair arrangement. Would Mr. Miller consider fifty-fifty?"

Deborah reacted quickly, "There is no way that Oscar Miller will accept a fifty-fifty arrangement. He wants complete control. He doesn't have faith in the business acumen of your clients."

Rusty laughed, "So that's a polite way of saying he thinks they're idiots?"

"I didn't say that at all," Deborah answered, attempting to show no emotion as she spoke. "They're in bankruptcy and they have made some bad decisions. Oscar doesn't know them well enough to form an opinion as to the level of their IQs. He will only go along with a plan like this if he is in complete control."

Neil Sherman wanted to try and get something going, "Well, complete control doesn't necessarily mean twenty-five/seventy-five. There are other ways to divide things up."

"I have to go," she responded. "My husband is in the lobby waiting for me. You speak to your clients and let me know what they have to say. But you should probably emphasize to them that if Oscar Miller doesn't have complete control of the club, there will never be a deal and the club will be torn down."

"What about fifty-one percent for the Millers?" Rusty asked quickly, trying to get a word in before Deborah hung up.

"Try sixty-two percent," Deborah said. "If your clients will accept that, I will try to sell it to Oscar. I don't think he would consider any percentage lower than sixty-two percent and I'm not really certain he'll even accept that."

Deborah had thrown out the sixty-two percent figure to see what reaction she might get; however, it seemed like a fairer percentage to her and she was pretty sure it would satisfy Oscar. She also thought that the beach club would probably turn a profit with Oscar at the helm. She was reasonably certain, given his business experience, that he could turn it into a money-making operation. From the little time she had spent with the club owners, she had come to the conclusion that they would always have money problems. She had the sense that left to their own resources, they would forever be chasing rainbows, attempting to impress club members by spending too much money on superficial items. Oscar would keep them on track.

Chapter Fourteen

January 1993

A committee was selected to begin interviewing for the position of Rabbi of Beth Torah, "*The* Synagogue" located on Long Island's famed North Shore. The committee struggled to come up with criteria they could all agree on before beginning their interviews.

Deborah appointed Barry Weinstein as Chair of the Rabbi's Search Committee. They discussed the importance of his listening to all points of view while not expressing his own.

"That doesn't sound hard," Barry assured her, greatly relieved at the notion that he would never have to express an opinion, and quite happy to have Deborah take the heat on this one. If things went wrong, he was prepared to jump in as a hero and take over, but given all that was going on it was much safer to keep himself removed from the controversy.

The first meeting of the new Rabbi's Search Committee turned out to be more eventful than Deborah or Barry would have expected. Shortly into the meeting Barry decided to have each person express what they felt was critical to look for in a Rabbi.

Simmy Monash was quick to pronounce the feelings of his constituency. "As the brotherhood representative on this committee, we insist upon hiring a devotee of our late, beloved Rabbi Levinson, a man who will continue in the sacred tradition of excellence that we have become accustomed to at Beth Torah." His voice broke as he spoke, and he emphasized his Mideastern accent, which he firmly believed made him sound more pious.

Rochelle Levy expressed the opinion of the Sisterhood. "Preserving the memory of our dearly beloved, brilliant, and very caring Rabbi

Levinson, we are interested in a dynamic man who will lead our children on the path of righteousness, emphasize Jewish study, and stimulate interest in our Sisterhood activities." The other Sisterhood representatives on the Committee applauded when she was done speaking.

Joyce Kaplan was quite clear in presenting the opinion of the YCC. "Our main thrust is to be certain that we hire a different kind of Rabbi, someone who is modern and forward-thinking, who will interpret Jewish law to include everyone and who will not sacrifice a large segment of our congregational family to some misguided prejudicial ideals written centuries ago."

Upon hearing her words Simmy Monash jumped up from his seat. "No respect. No respect," he shouted, "for our beloved Rabbi who is sitting at the side of the angels, looking down on us. You bring shame to the memory of his name and to all members of this sacred synagogue."

"I don't care where he's sitting now," replied Joyce Kaplan. "I only care about who we're replacing him with, and thank God he's gone! And if you ask me—"

"No one's asking," shouted Simmy.

"This committee is asking," she shouted back, "and I'm telling. All I have to say is we'd better select someone who is sensitive to the needs of women, or a lot of us are leaving."

"Good riddance. Go," Simmy said, pounding his fist on the table.

"Enough, Simmy," Rochelle proclaimed, firmly but calmly. "Sit down. She's entitled to have an opinion. You don't agree? Fine, but she's entitled to speak her mind. It's enough already."

Simmy's face was turning red with rage. "She's not entitled to defile our beloved Rabbi's memory," he continued shouting. "And you, you can't fool me, with that phony, sweet manner of yours. We all know that you agree with everything these crazy spoiled brats are asking for."

Up until this moment Harry had been sitting as usual at Rochelle's side, quietly listening to everything being said. "Simmy, don't talk to my wife in that tone of voice. Shut up or I'll squash you up into pulp."

Harry had never before exhibited such an outburst at the synagogue— but then no one had ever spoken to Rochelle with such disrespect either.

"It's okay, Harry," Rochelle responded, resting her hand on his shoulder. "Don't get excited, he's not worth it."

Deborah interrupted. "Excuse me, Simmy, but other people also want to have an opportunity to express what they think is important. Thank you for your opinion. We've all heard what you have to say. And, Harry, you're sitting here as a guest. Please don't abuse that privilege."

"Yes, this is a large committee. We must move on," Barry declared. Mumbling under his breath that they would never be able to agree on anything.

Deborah left the meeting feeling extraordinarily depressed. How were they ever going to resolve their problems?

Chapter Fifteen

January 1993

The next morning Brian and Seth called to say they would be performing at Tumbling Ted's, a club located near Union Square in Manhattan. "This place is hot, Mom," Brian said, sounding jubilant. "Agents come to find new talent here. If we're lucky we might get a few more gigs out of this."

"Well, your father and I will come to see you. We'll bring Grandma and Ben and Aunt Rose, Uncle Jacob, everyone. Make us proud."

There was a moment of silence and Brian finally spoke up, "Mom please don't misunderstand, but do you really think Grandma and Ben and Aunt Rose and Uncle Jacob will enjoy being in a club like this? The noise will be deafening."

"Are you kidding, they won't care about anything except how proud they are of you. Why would you take that pleasure away from them?"

"Oh, it's okay, Mom," Seth chimed in. They were apparently both on a speaker phone. "They'll be fine. Grandma will probably get everyone dancing. Don't worry about it, Brian."

Seth was the peacemaker in their family. He always wanted everyone to be happy.

"Ugh," Brian sighed. "I hope they don't say anything stupid."

"And since when do they say stupid things?" Deborah asked.

"You've got to be kidding. How often do you talk to Uncle Jacob? You ask him about soap and he'll tell you about door handles."

"That's because he doesn't hear well and he's too embarrassed to keep asking you to repeat what you're saying so he pretends to hear and then he tries to answer you and his answers often don't make sense because he has no idea of what you were asking. But he still does the *New York Times* crossword puzzle every morning. There's no grass growing under his feet. And listening to music is still one of his greatest pleasures."

"Oh, all right," Brian sighed. "I can see this is not a battle I'm going to win."

"Nor should you," Deborah answered, clearly disturbed by her son's attitude. "This is your family and they love you. You're lucky to have them. You should count your blessings and be happy that they're still alive and able and thrilled to give you support." Deborah could feel herself holding back tears.

"All right, all right, I'm sorry. Goodbye. I'll talk to you tomorrow." Brian hung up and Deborah was shocked and saddened by his insensitivity.

"He's young. He has to learn to think about what he's saying before he opens his mouth," Carl told her when she repeated her conversation with Brian to him. "Don't worry about it. I'm sure Brian has already forgotten the conversation."

"Maybe," Deborah replied. She had spent her entire life protecting her mother and her aunt and uncle from the world around them; had the time really come when she had to protect them from her own children?

"You're overreacting," Carl insisted. "It's over, forget about it."

"I'll try for now," she answered, "but I hope I never hear anything like that from Brian again. I don't understand how he could grow up in our house and still be so insensitive to their feelings."

"He's not going to do it again," Carl assured her, and Deborah knew instantly that he was planning on speaking to both their sons to ensure that Brian would watch his words more carefully in the future.

"I'm really disappointed in him," Deborah answered.

"They're just young," Carl smiled and hugged her. Carl knew that Brian had to understand the difference between his family and his friends' families. For Deborah and her family, Brian and Seth were their answer to the Holocaust—proof that Hitler didn't win. Their children were the survivors' revenge. Brian might have slipped for a moment, but there was no way that he didn't really understand his role in the family dynamics.

The air in Tumbling Ted's was thick with the sweet smell of incense. It was an exciting evening for Deborah and her entourage, noisy, and certainly different from any place they had ever been to before. If Brina, Ben, Uncle

Jacob, and Aunt Rose felt uncomfortable, it was certainly not obvious from looking at them. They smiled at everyone, slowly sipping their drinks, being chatty and friendly while beaming with pride. Ben told everyone who would listen that they were here to see Brian and Seth.

Brina was very busy observing the other people in the room, all of whom were very young, and casually dressed. Almost everyone was wearing jeans with a variety of different tops and accessories. There were various types of looks. Some were punky with green or pink hair; there was one group who were dressed in black and seemed to be prepared for a pending funeral. There were groups of young men and women flirting with each other while attempting to appear nonchalant. For the most part, the crowd was filled with twenty-somethings out to have a good time.

Brina wasn't sure what to focus on first. Her eyes kept jumping from one part of the room to another, one table to another, attempting to breathe in the essence of the experience of just being there. She was determined to do her best to enjoy herself, no matter how loud the music was.

When the M.C. announced Brian and Seth's group, Deborah's family screamed like teenagers. Their enthusiasm was so contagious that with some encouragement from Uncle Jacob, the tables around them also began to scream, and BS Rocks got the loudest ovation of any of the groups that had performed up until that point. Brian and Seth smiled in their direction, "Nothing like bringing Mom and Grandma down to cheer you on," Seth shouted into the microphone before beginning their routine. Everyone screamed even louder. Seth and Brian laughed and they began.

Deborah grew up listening to and playing sweet melodies that were soothing to the ear. Since they were no longer living at home, it had been a while since she had heard Brian and Seth play, and their musical style had definitely matured. There was a loud beat that could seem almost irritating; however it was softened by the effect of the violin that they had also managed to incorporate into their music and there were sections where Brian did a violin solo as part of the musical arrangement and that made what they played more recognizable to her. Deborah was surprised at how comfortably they carried themselves up on the stage.

Their group consisted of a young man on the piano, a drummer, Seth on the guitar, Brian on the violin, a tenor sax and two attractive young women who sang in the background and swayed to the music. It was an interesting combination of instruments, which made for an interesting sound. Seth sang a solo while moving about with his guitar, and the two young women hummed in back of him. No more the little boys she used to carpool around the neighborhood. How had the years gone by so quickly? Deborah remembered her own childhood as a painful endurance test that enveloped her, and the shadow that it cast would last forever, but the time spent mothering her own children, that was a happy time in her life, but it passed too quickly, and in the blink of an eye it was over.

Her sons had flown away from the nest and they were quite busy pursuing their own future. If Brian was less sensitive than she would have hoped, there wasn't much she could do about that anymore. All she could do is hope that she had shown her sons how to make good choices for themselves in life and pray that they would use common sense while following their dreams. They would never understand in the same way she did that their music was a link in the chain that tied them to her father, the grandfather they never knew. If it was possible for her father to be looking down at them, Deborah knew that watching them perform on stage, he also must be beaming with pride.

Chapter Sixteen

February 1993

The morning newspaper headline read: "Police Still Seeking Clues in Murder of Prominent Rabbi."

Simmy Monash believed that his position as Brotherhood President required him to stop by the synagogue at least once a day. He carried the same message with him each time he arrived, "What are the police doing with our tax money if they can't even find out who killed our *Tsadik*?"

Though it had become very difficult, Deborah tried to focus on the issues of the day-to-day running of the synagogue. At some point she knew that since Esther was living in a synagogue-owned house, she would have to be asked to move out. However, that wouldn't be a problem until a new Rabbi was hired, and Deborah prayed that Esther would see the light without having to be prodded.

Rabbi Nachum Klein, the interim Rabbi, was a pleasant enough man, perfectly willing to officiate at weddings, funerals, and prayer services, but he made it quite clear that he had absolutely no interest in involving himself in the day-to-day operations of the synagogue. An immediate problem confronting Deborah was that Rabbi Klein had showed up two days early to move his things into the Rabbi's study, and Leon Feldman had thrown him out, calling him a "trespasser." Rabbi Klein was demanding an apology.

"The body isn't cold yet," Leon shouted at Deborah. "We haven't even cleaned out Rabbi Levinson's desk and this interloper is here moving himself in. What's the matter? He couldn't wait a day or two? Who the hell does he think he is?"

"He knows who he is, Leon: he's a Rabbi who we've hired to do a job, and he deserves to be treated with respect. You have to apologize to him for the way you behaved," Deborah answered calmly, hoping to get him to stop shouting.

"Me apologize to that free loader? Are you kidding? He walks in here, helps himself to a little of everything, like he really belongs, and you think I should apologize? No way, lady. No how, no way!"

"Leon, stop shouting at me, because I will not tolerate it. I am telling you that Rabbi Klein is a member of our Synagogue family for the next six months, and if you don't treat him with respect, you will have to suffer the consequences, and don't make me spell out what those are. He is a Rabbi and he is our guest, and I don't care how you do it, but you make him feel welcome, and you are to do it now."

Deborah never raised her voice, but her tone was quite stern and Leon Feldman was surprised enough not to respond.

Detective Brody was in touch with her regularly to inform her that they had not yet gotten a break on the case, but he was sure one would come soon. The last time he called he asked her not to make any staff changes at the synagogue without speaking to him first. She couldn't help but wonder if Leon had related their last discussion, hoping to get some sympathy.

In all the years Deborah had known Benjamin Franklin Lieb, she had never spent more than five minutes with him away from her mother at any one time. His recent call, wanting to meet her for lunch, had to have great significance, and rather than adding to the suspense in her life she decided to meet him that very day. She had grown fond of Ben over the years, and she would always be grateful for his financial help, but for all of that, she and Ben barely knew each other. He was today what he had always been: her mother's manfriend, a person whose arrival in her mother's life had made her own life considerably better in many ways. Ben took care of her mother financially and spent his time trying to make her happy.

They made plans to meet at Crabby Davey's, a popular seafood restaurant on Long Island Sound. Crabby Davey's was pricey for dinner, but reasonable for lunch, and Deborah met clients there quite often. Ben, being somewhat compulsive, generally was at least ten minutes early for any engagement, so Deborah was careful to be at the restaurant on time, but to her surprise he had not yet arrived. She sat at a small, round table overlooking the once-beautiful, now-polluted Sound, sipping a glass of club soda and glancing up at the entrance every now and then to look for him.

"I'm sorry I'm late," Ben whispered, dashing to the table, apparently out of breath. He leaned over and kissed her lightly on the cheek. Deborah was brought back to the present. In spite of his years, Ben was still a handsome man. "The parking lot attendants all think they're junior Mario Andrettis in training. I wanted to watch them park my car to make sure they didn't run it into the Sound. Unfortunately, they didn't seem to be in any hurry."

"No problem," Deborah smiled. "I haven't been here very long," she lied.

"Before we speak about anything else, I can't believe what's going on at your synagogue. You have got to tell me what's really happening with this murder."

"Not much different than what you see in the newspapers, I don't think. It's hard to imagine who would do such a thing, and the police don't seem to have a clue either, as far as I can see."

This couldn't possibly be what he wanted to speak to her about, could it? Ben continued to ask her questions about Rabbi Levinson and the synagogue, until the waiter took their food order, and then, he rather abruptly changed the subject.

"You must be wondering why I wanted to speak to you."

"Yes, I guess I am," she responded without any hesitation.

"Even as a child, you were always discrete. You never asked me any questions. I showed up one day and you just accepted me as part of your life. I have always considered that rather remarkable."

"I accepted you as part of my mother's life," Deborah corrected him. "You made her happy and that was very important to me."

"I tried to make you happy too," Ben sighed, sounding a bit discouraged.

"I don't know if you can understand this, but as a child, no one could make me happy. It was my job to make everyone else happy. I've been seventy years old almost since the day I was born, and it's taken me all these years and two children of my own to get that much self-understanding," Deborah revealed.

"Yes, I always knew that. I don't think I ever saw you behave like a child."

"I had no childhood," Deborah spoke softly.

"That's so sad," he replied.

"It was perhaps a unique time in the history of the world and things were very different than they are today. I did what I had to do. I've always felt loved. I had and still have strong, wonderful people around me who have always been great role models. I have a good life now, and everything worked out fine. But this can't be what you want to speak to me about, I don't imagine."

"Not really. After all these years, it's suddenly important that you learn more about me and my other life," Ben stated while showing little emotion. "I know you must realize that I have another family."

"I suppose I do, but it's just one of those things I thought I was happier not knowing about," she commented. Part of her was hoping he would not continue. "My mother didn't seem concerned, so I wasn't either."

"Well, your mamma knows the truth. She could have told you at any time, but she also, for whatever reason, chose not to."

Deborah smiled, "That's how we are, my Mother and I. No one could be closer than we are, but we're careful about what we tell each other."

"Well, I'm also careful about what I tell your mamma, that's why I want to talk to you now. First, I want you to know that I do have a wife, but she is an invalid. I have two sons, who are very important to me. I know I used to mention them to you from time to time." Ben watched carefully to see if he could detect her reaction, but Deborah was well practiced at remaining calm no matter what was being said around her. "My wife, Lenore, she had a stroke giving birth to my younger son," he continued. "She always was a passive soul, not someone to fight back, and she's been an invalid for all these years. The right side of her body is paralyzed and she's in a wheelchair. She barely speaks and makes no effort to do anything but cry over her wretched fate.

"Over the years I've had her to many doctors, therapists, shrinks—you name it, we've been there. But she is depressed and she has chosen to make no attempt to get better nor to do anything other than sit in a wheelchair all day, and we don't have much of a relationship.

"I was a very young man when all of this happened, and as time went on I began to feel desperate. I needed a real companion, someone I could be connected to both physically and spiritually, but I couldn't bring myself to leave Lenore. She is, after all, the mother of my children."

"Do your sons know about my mother?" Deborah asked.

"Not yet. They probably suspect the truth. They're not babies any longer and they're certainly not stupid, but I thought it was best to keep things separate. However, now there's a problem."

Deborah continued listening.

"There's no easy way to break this news, but I have stomach cancer and while I am going to begin treatment next week, I have to face reality now."

Deborah felt her body suddenly stiffen. "My God, Ben." What was she supposed to say?

Her hand was resting on the table and he took hold of it gently, "Shah," he said. "It's okay. Years ago I put aside a trust fund for your mother in the event that something suddenly happened to me. Neither of us are kids anymore, and I don't know how much time she has left on this earth, but there's enough to take care of her and to help your aunt and uncle a little bit too." Ben obviously had planned out very carefully what he had to do and what he would say.

"I will, of course, have to tell my sons what I have done, because it would be terrible for them to find out after I die. For everything else that has happened, financially God has been good to me in my lifetime; I've made money, I invested it wisely, and my children should be more than happy with what I've left them. The biggest problem for them will be caring for Lenore, but I have set up a trust fund for her also. I can only pray they will give her the attention that she requires.

"I expect that my children will respect my feelings, but just in case they don't, and this is where you come in, I've brought a copy of my will and the papers relating to the trust funds. I want you to look everything over to make sure it's all the way it's supposed to be or the way you think it should be. I also want you to be very familiar with every detail, just to be certain that all of my wishes are carried out."

"Have you discussed any of this with my mother?" Deborah inquired, feeling profoundly saddened by all of what Ben had revealed.

"Brina has suffered so much in her life. How can I tell her?" Ben's voice cracked as he spoke.

"How could you not tell her?" Deborah gasped.

"I don't know, I'm just afraid she will not be able to handle it. I've tried to protect her all these years, but this, I just don't know."

"No matter what you think, my mother is strong. Many of the other women who found themselves in her situation during the war gave up and died. My mother not only managed to live as a partisan, but she survived Treblinka. Don't you worry, she can handle any curve life throws her way. You've given to her all these years, don't deprive her of the opportunity to give back, because I think that would really destroy her."

Ben smiled. "Didn't you just get finished telling me that you've also always protected your mother?"

"It's not the same thing. You're not me. I tried to make my mother happy. That was my own doing. I also tried to make my aunt and uncle happy. To some extent I still do that, but we were all strangers in a new country, and we had a sad history. We had to keep propping each other up. That's how we survived. They lived through me because here in America I had opportunities they never had. They all may be vulnerable on some level, but that doesn't mean they break easily.

"Right now you need my mother, and God knows she needs you, so let her help. It's important that you allow her to be there for you." Deborah felt emotionally drained.

"I'll think about what you're saying, but in the meantime, you can pay me back for all those years of law school by making sure I have all my papers in order."

"I wish it wasn't necessary for me to do this, but you know I will. And in case I haven't told you lately, thank you for law school, it was one of the most significant things you ever could have done for me, and I know there was no way we could have managed it financially without you."

"You're welcome, but somehow I'm sure you would have found a way."

Chapter Seventeen

February 1993

O n her way back to the office Deborah stopped by Beth Torah. She wanted to go into the sanctuary to pray for Ben, and while she was there she would sign the payroll checks. She was surprised to see Detective Brody's car parked by the front door. She found him sitting in Leon Feldman's office looking through a small, black loose-leaf book.

"Hi. Anything new?" she asked, bounding into the room.

"Actually, lots of things," he smiled at her.

"Really? That sounds promising," she said, obviously intrigued by his response.

"You see this little black book right here?" he said, pointing to a small loose-leaf binder on the desk. "This belonged to your Rabbi. It's just chock-full of all kinds of interesting tidbits of information."

"Like what?" she asked.

"Well, Rabbi Levinson, it appears, was keeping tabs on some of his congregants. I can only assume with the intent of blackmailing them into cooperation at some later date. His head may have been filled with prayer, but I would say his two feet were firmly planted in reality."

"Where did you find that?" Deborah was astonished.

"Oh, the Rabbi's mother has been most cooperative. I am reasonably sure, in fact, that to a great extent it was she who had been his eyes and ears into the hidden secrets of your Temple family, and apparently very little escaped her prudent vigil. She does assure me, though, that he picked up information from other sources as well."

"My God, that sweet little old lady. I can't believe it."

"Perhaps she is a sweet little old lady, and perhaps she's not, but in this case she was a mother protecting her only son, and she was seeing to it that he was well armed with a small arsenal of information. If words could kill, we've got another Hiroshima right here in this book."

Detective Brody clearly found the situation somewhat amusing, but Deborah felt as though she had just been through shock therapy. "So, what happens next?" she asked.

"I have made some appointments to talk to people whose names and situations are outlined in this book. We'll have to see where that takes us."

"I guess you're not prepared to share that with the Prez of the congregation?" she teased.

"Maybe I am, but not right at this moment. Joyce Kaplan is due in to see me momentarily, and from the little bit we spoke on the phone, I think it may be a somewhat stormy meeting."

"Joyce Kaplan? Well, I'm sure there's plenty he would have wanted to write about her. Maybe I'm naive, but how do you know any of that stuff is true?"

"I don't. I can use my judgment after speaking with the people themselves. But Joyce Kaplan, in case you aren't aware, did have a key to this building."

"I guess as the leader of the Young Couples Club she was entitled to one. I hadn't thought about it before. Sorry I didn't give you her name myself. But that doesn't mean she killed the Rabbi."

"Of course not, but it does make her one of several suspects."

"I think I hear her voice, I'd better leave. When can I talk to you about that book?"

"Call me in the morning. I should be in my office. Maybe we can meet for breakfast or lunch."

"You've got a date."

Deborah left, still stunned by the thought of the Rabbi's keeping a diary of information. She couldn't imagine why he would want to be blackmailing congregants. There had to be a reason why Rabbi Levinson was doing this.

Brian and Seth had called Deborah's office to give her the latest schedule of clubs they would be performing at and to tell her that they would be appearing on a local telethon on cable TV, raising money for multiple sclerosis the next Sunday evening.

"How did the people running the telethon hear about you?" Deborah had inquired.

"We joined sort of a club, a group of men and women who are children of Holocaust survivors. Someone in that group recommended us."

"You felt the need to join a group of survivors' children?"

"Yeah, well, it's good to have people to talk to who understand where we're coming from, you know?" Seth replied. "Why? Would that upset you?"

"No, it doesn't upset me," Deborah quickly responded, knowing that in some kind of way it did make her uncomfortable, but she wasn't sure exactly why. "And if they're helping you in your career, I'm certainly glad you joined."

"We didn't join for that reason," Brian jumped in. "It's just that sometimes it seems to me, and I think Seth agrees, we feel like we have been brought up to see the world differently than most people do, and there are times when we need to talk to others who see the world as we do, sort of a support group."

"Sure, I understand that," Deborah lied. "Don't worry, your father and I will be watching you. I'll call everyone I know and ask them to tune in."

"And tell them to donate," said Seth.

"I certainly will."

Deborah and Carl were having dinner at the local diner. Deborah was repeating to Carl her conversation with Brian and Seth.

"I don't know why I'm upset that our children feel different and think they need to have a support group to help them. I guess maybe I didn't do such a good job as a mother."

Carl took her hand. "No, you were a wonderful mother," he responded. "Everyone is unique, but you are more unique than most. You're more sensitive, more involved with your family, and perhaps a bit more determined than the mothers of our sons' friends. I am certain that they feel your pain, and they admire your determination. The fact that they're seeking out like-minded people is nothing for you to be upset about. They're looking for more self-understanding.

"Okay, I'll buy into what you're saying," Deborah smiled, not knowing if she agreed with him or not.

"And did anything happen at the Temple today that I should know about?"

Deborah began to fill him in on the excitement concerning the Rabbi's black book.

"So, you see, Carl, this goes back to my theory that you never really know people the way you think you know them." Deborah was sipping a Diet Coke while ranting on about the Rabbi's diary.

"That's unbelievable. You mean to say Rabbi Levinson actually had a little black book?" Carl was smiling from ear to ear. "Talk about weird! And the thought of his mother running around peeping into keyholes, it's incredible! It's like something out of a movie."

"A B-movie maybe," Deborah grumbled. "I have to admit though that Sonia Levinson has very good people skills. Everyone likes her. Rochelle has told me that she's on loads of committees and she works very hard for Sisterhood. I guess she was in a position to hear a lot of gossip, or maybe people just confided in her. We'll probably never know!"

"'People skills.' Now that's something Esther could have worked a little harder at," Carl muttered, still smiling.

"Carl, that's not true and it's not fair for you to say that," said Deborah, sounding somewhat annoyed. "She's a social worker. She's got to have people skills. I just think she didn't have synagogue skills. I think it's obvious that she didn't give a damn. It's like this was his thing, so let him have it, and since he had his mother to fill in for her, it worked out well for all of them. I wonder if Esther knew about his little black book?"

"Maybe she was giving him information too."

"Never!" Deborah exclaimed with conviction. "Esther handled things head-on. It would be totally out of character for her to keep track of gossip in that way."

"So are you going to call an executive meeting about this? I can't wait to hear about Simmy's reaction."

Deborah laughed. "I know what you mean. But no, I don't think I'll mention this just yet. Everyone will get upset worrying about whether or not they're in the book. We'll just see what happens."

Deborah and Carl arrived home to find three very agitated messages from Joyce Kaplan on the answer machine. "Deborah, call me back immediately. No matter what time you get home."

"She really does sound stressed out. I bet there was something very interesting in that book about her," Deborah picked up the phone and began dialing.

"Hi, Joyce, this is Deborah. Is everything okay?"

"Okay? No, everything is not okay. That little weasel of a Rabbi. Did you know he was keeping a diary filled with sordid information he could use as blackmail?" Joyce was screaming in a loud, shrill voice.

Deborah pulled the phone away from her ear. "I just heard about that today from Detective Brody. I think that's a recent discovery."

"Well, let me assure you that no matter who I'm sleeping with, I would never have killed that contemptible sneak, certainly not with a bullet. A quick death was too good for him. If I had done it, I would have removed his skin layer by layer and watched him squirm. That's what he deserved. Torture! If someone wants to ruin my marriage by telling this bullshit to Fred, so be it, but imagine that Rabbi, that two-faced snake in the grass, prancing around as though he was holier than everyone and all the while he was getting vicarious kicks and thriving off of the lust of those people who looked up to him and trusted him as a man of God."

Joyce's voice was piercing, her pitch was at least five octaves higher than usual. Carl was leaning against her and could hear everything that was being said.

"Who was she sleeping with?" he whispered with the excitement of a sexually aroused sixteen-year-old.

Deborah shrugged. "I'm sorry, Joyce, I don't know anything about what's in the book, honestly. All I know is that the book exists. That's all Detective Brody told me."

"Don't worry, you'll be hearing, I'm sure. But I want you to explain to that dickhead Brody that I don't shoot people. It just isn't necessary. I can get everything I want done without going to jail. I may have wished him dead, but I sure as hell didn't kill him."

"Why don't you tell that to Detective Brody yourself?" Deborah was speaking calmly, hoping that she could sooth some of Joyce's ruffled feathers.

"Don't you think I told him that? But do you think he believed me?" Joyce's voice was raspy and cracking. "He's got a whole history of my relationship with Lester Calderon written in that fucking book; he knows I have a key to the synagogue and that I hated the holy bastard. What is he supposed to think?"

"I doubt that you're the only one in that situation." At the mention of Lester Calderon's name it was all Deborah could do to contain herself. "That book is obviously filled with information on lots of people, and you were hardly the only one in the synagogue who was upset with the Rabbi, so relax. If you didn't do it, you didn't do it. Detective Brody is looking for the person who did do it."

"No, he's not. You can't be that naive. That's not how this shit works and you of all people have got to know that. He's looking for someone to offer up to his bosses and the media, to get everyone off his own back. Who really did it is not relevant. Well, I'm not about to become anyone's sacrificial lamb."

"Of course not," Deborah assured her. "Like I said, I'm sure you're not alone in this. I think you'd best rest your voice though, or you're not going to be able to speak at all by tomorrow."

"Yeah, sure. But can you believe it? That devout piece of shit. Where the hell did he get all of this information from? I didn't think he ever got his head out of that fucking *siddur* he carried around. He must have had spies out among the masses. Think of it, some old farts crawling around motel rooms examining the dirty sheets. It's disgusting!"

"Good night, Joyce. I'll speak to you tomorrow. Get some rest."

"I'll try, but I need you to speak to that detective for me. I don't want him coming around here and scaring my kids."

Deborah put the phone back on the end table. "Lester Calderon," she sighed, "I never would have believed it."

"Isn't his wife her best friend?" Carl asked.

"Yes, I think so. I guess anybody who looks like Lester Calderon would be having an affair with somebody," she said so quietly that she didn't think Carl could hear her.

"Rita Calderon ain't exactly a dog, you know, but Joyce Kaplan? Compared to Rita, she's living in the Bronx Zoo," Carl commented.

"If that isn't just like a man. Did it ever occur to you that Rita's IQ is so low she couldn't find her way into the bedroom without a guide dog? Maybe he was attracted to Joyce's intelligence."

Carl began laughing uncontrollably. "Oh, sure, that's right. Les is sleeping with Joyce so he can check out her opinions on world events. Now I've heard everything!" He was bent over, holding his stomach.

Deborah grabbed a pillow off the bed and threw it at him. "Shut up. I hate it when you sound just like a man."

"I can't help it," Carl said, wrestling her onto the bed. "That's what I am—one of the beasts."

"You are a beast," she whispered, succumbing to the moment and pulling him on top of her. The Rabbi was dead and Ben was dying, but life, after all, does go on.

The next morning Deborah called Detective Brody. He was busy, but told her he would stop by her office sometime later in the day. True to his word, at 2:30 her secretary buzzed to tell her he had arrived.

"You sure know how to keep someone in suspense," she smiled.

"Well, this may be the most pressing case I'm working on, but there are still a few other homicides happening in the greater community that need my attention from time to time."

"Well, thank goodness. How else could criminal attorneys earn a living?" Deborah quipped. "You mean to say you didn't spend the morning interviewing more people listed in that little black book?"

"No, I haven't sorted it all out yet," he answered.

Deborah noticed that a stray curl had broken loose from Detective Brody's otherwise well-groomed hair; it was hanging down on his forehead. There was an energy about him that made him appear almost like a mischievous little boy, rather than the grown man that he was.

"Joyce Kaplan called me last night. She was quite upset. She believes she is a real suspect now in this case, and she wants me to assure you of her innocence."

"Well, she certainly can't be ruled out at this stage of the game, not given the facts that we have."

"Are you going to tell her husband about Lester?" Deborah asked.

"Oh, she told you," he said without surprise. "Not yet, and not unless I think it's necessary for some reason or other. It's not my desire to break up anyone's marriage, although if she's sleeping around maybe there isn't much to break up. I'm just trying to find the murderer."

"Isn't it possible that the real killer had nothing to do with the synagogue at all?"

"Anything is possible, but at this point I would think that's highly unlikely. There are any number of people who might have wanted to see the Rabbi dead for a whole variety of reasons, and many of them are in this little book over here."

"Am I in that book?" she asked, wondering what the Rabbi and his mother could possibly have said about her.

"No, not you," he smiled. "You managed to escape untainted. But I would like to go over some of what is here in confidence with you. You do know the cast of characters and I don't, and I could use some insight."

"Of course. I'm here to help, and I'm also dying of curiosity."

"Of course anything I say to you, I assume is in confidence. We understand that."

"But of course. Does that include Carl?" she asked.

"No. I consider the two of you as aides in this case, but no one else is to know unless they speak of it themselves."

"Absolutely," she answered in her most solemn tone of voice.

"You mentioned Simmy Monash the other day. Well apparently your instincts on him were not unfounded. Mr. Monash has indeed made his money in leasing, but it appears as though some of the leasing he's handling are porn theaters in Manhattan, and he maintains some sort of an interest in them. He apparently had a similar business in Iran and barely escaped with his life when the fanatics came to power."

"Porn theaters," Deborah gasped. "But he appears to be so religious. It doesn't seem possible. Have you checked this all out? How do you know that the things written in that book aren't just allegations, delusions of a deranged old lady and her paranoid son?"

"Oh, no, we're still probing, but anything I mention to you has been checked out, and it's real, all right? He wouldn't be the first person who managed to separate religion and real life into two distinctly different categories. As you must know, it happens every day of the week. And your Mr. Monash has had a number of arrests for impairing the morals of a minor, among other things—just trivial scars of his trade—but he has thus far managed to avoid jail time."

"But he was one of the Rabbi's staunchest supporters. The Rabbi and he were great buddies, it's interesting that there would be information on him in that book."

"I suspect that the Rabbi's mother is a better judge of character than the Rabbi was, and from what she tells us, she is the one who gave the Rabbi a good deal of the information to put into the book. I suppose when push comes to shove, Sonia Levinson didn't trust Simmy Monash, and it is also quite possible that the Rabbi was so outraged at learning of Simmy's line of work that he confronted him with the information, which then, clearly, could make Simmy Monash a suspect too.

"Incidentally, you wouldn't happen to know if anyone owed the Rabbi a large sum of money, would you?"

Deborah was startled. "I didn't think the Rabbi had large sums of money to be lending out to anyone. No, I'm not aware that anyone owed him money. But then again I was hardly his confidant."

"Well, there apparently was some money due to somebody, I assume to the Rabbi himself, although that is only an assumption. Under any circumstances, he was keeping track of the money. I found a record of payments on a ledger-type pad that he had hidden at the bottom of his bookcase. There's no identification of who or what it is, just an itemization of funds. Up until his death, he was being repaid at the rate of seven hundred fifty dollars a month. It appears as if the last month had not been paid. And it's odd that he would have hidden it away in such an obscure place."

"Maybe it was paid in full and he hadn't bothered to enter the last payment into his records. Isn't that possible?" asked Deborah.

"Of course it's possible. Anything is possible. I would like to find out who the debtor is, though."

"Have you asked Esther or Sonia, his mother, about it? Maybe he mentioned something to one of them."

"I did ask his mother, but she apparently doesn't know anything about it. I haven't had a chance to talk to Esther yet. We just began to study the ledger book yesterday."

"Are there any other shocking tidbits you have to offer?" Deborah asked.

"Well, it's pretty clear that Rita and Lester Calderon had an open marriage, but that might have been obvious to anyone as perceptive as you are. They, of course, have each had any number of partners both in and out of your synagogue family. The partners are listed in the diary alphabetically."

How could Deborah explain to this man that nothing of a sexual nature was obvious to her? For all that she had lived through as a child and all she had accomplished in her career, when it came to anything even slightly erotic, in truth, she was today as she had always been: the sheltered child of a Holocaust survivor, protected first by her mother, her Aunt Rose, and Uncle Jake, and now by the only man she had ever dated or had any physical relationship with at all, her husband. No, she had not noticed that Rita and Les Calderon had an open marriage. What she had noticed was that Rita Calderon was beautiful and sensual like her own mother, and that even Carl couldn't help but take notice when she was anywhere in sight. Deborah suddenly felt like an awkward schoolgirl once again, unable to fit into the world around her.

"Is anything wrong?" Detective Brody asked, sensing the change in her mood.

"No, it's just sad to see how people choose to lead their lives, I guess."

"Well, I certainly can't disagree with that."

"Are there many more skeletons bobbing up and down in Beth Torah's closet?"

"Maybe a few more, but nothing yet that would bring on a crime of passion, which is what we are assuming this was. For example, Rochelle Levy's son was apparently in a homosexual relationship, but that's kind of mild stuff for the nineties."

"It may be mild stuff, but Rochelle has never spoken of it so I have to assume it's somewhat of a touchy subject for her."

"Touchy enough to kill for?" asked the detective.

"Who knows? None of this stuff seems like it's enough to kill for. Nevertheless, the man is dead. Do you think Rochelle did it?"

"I'm not rushing to judgment just yet."

"In the greater scheme of things, she is an unlikely suspect, but then, who am I to say?"

"Well, we're still in the process of verifying what the Rabbi has written. We can talk about it again when I've had a chance to verify some more of what's in this book. But tell me, what do you think about Rita and Lester Calderon as suspects?

"I don't know either one of them well enough to think anything. They're both sexy, beautiful people. Rita and Joyce Kaplan are close friends. Joyce tells her when to jump, and Rita asks, 'How high?' That's all I know."

"And Simmy Monash," the detective asked, trying unsuccessfully to keep himself from smiling.

"Well, I've always suspected he was a slimeball, and now I can be sure he is, but murder? I don't know. He really did seem to adore the Rabbi. It's hard to figure."

"I know. They're all hard to figure," Detective Brody mumbled.

The evening Newspaper Headline read: "New Clues in Murder of Popular Rabbi," along with the following quote:

> "We are much closer to finding the Rabbi's murderer," says Detective Brody, who is heading up the taskforce of detectives working on the case.

Chapter Eighteen

February 1993

It was Deborah and Susan King's custom to meet at least once a month to share ideas and opinions on the world around them. Lately all of their conversations centered around Rabbi Levinson's murder.

"With all the publicity this case is getting, I can't believe the police haven't been able to come up with a suspect," Susan pronounced, lifting up her beer mug. "It's very strange."

"Well, the clues don't seem to be there, and it's hard to figure out." Deborah brought her up to date, trusting her with more information than she would consider passing on to anyone other than Carl.

"Murdering your Rabbi is an incredible thought. There are very profound sentiments involved. People feel for their Rabbis, ministers, and priests in much the same fashion as they do their lovers. There's a tremendous range of emotion involved, all of it intense. Find someone who loved him or hated him with great passion, and that's probably your best suspect."

Deborah laughed. "That's almost the entire congregation."

"Are you sure? Expressing like or dislike for his views is one thing, but passion is something else. Passion is obsessive, it envelops you completely. I've defended many people who have committed crimes of passion over the years, and there's a commonality that I've learned to look for in speaking to them. A fervor, if you will, that distinguishes them from other suspects in the case."

"I'll try to keep that in mind, but at this point, I still think it could be half the congregation.

"To change the subject for a moment, I'd like to tell you about a dream I had," Deborah blurted out suddenly. She had no idea why she was divulging this to Susan.

"A dream? Okay." Susan sat waiting for her to continue.

"The only person I've mentioned this to is Carl. I'm afraid to tell anyone else, but you know me well enough to know that I am not crazy."

"Boy, this must be some dream! I can hardly wait to hear it." Susan moved forward in her chair.

"What if I told you that at his moment of death, Rabbi Levinson came to speak to me?"

If Susan King was surprised by what Deborah had to say, she masked it well. "What could I say?" she asked. "Or what would you like me to say?"

"I don't know what I would like you to say, but Carl thinks it was nothing but a dream. I can't believe that Rabbi Levinson appearing to me at the exact moment of his death doesn't have some significance."

"Did he speak to you at all?"

"No. He tried to speak, but I couldn't hear him. He was hovering over my bed. I don't know if possibly he was asking me to avenge his death. You know, there is a Kabbalistic belief I remember reading about at one point. It's something like his spirit will be roaming around the world until his deeds have been resolved. Do you think that's at all possible?"

"I don't know what is or is not possible. However, if it makes you feel better, I can tell you that you are not the only person who has ever had such a revelation."

"You know other people who have had similar experiences?" Deborah asked, overcome by feelings of relief and amazement at the same time.

"In my career, I have had two clients tell me of visits they had received from the great beyond. And I have, on rare occasions, used the services of psychics to try and uncover crime-related information. I have no opinion on the veracity of any of it, but I've lived long enough to know that we all have a lot to learn. Just follow your own instincts and you won't go wrong."

"I wish Carl was as open as you are. He insists that I have an overactive imagination."

Susan laughed. "Well, I think men react very differently than women to unexplained phenomena. If you expect him to agree that any kind of psychic occurrence has some basis in fact, then you're a lot more of a dreamer than I know you to be."

"It's strange how things are. I hadn't expected to tell you about this before I started talking about it, and I began blurting it all out before I understood why I was telling you, but I suppose I instinctively knew you would understand. Thank you. For the first time since all this happened, I feel at least somewhat secure that I didn't have a hallucination."

"We've known each other a long time," Susan smiled reassuringly. "If we managed to survive as law students in NYU at the time we did, there's little else that we can't get through together, or alone when necessary. Let me know if I can be of help—and you know I'm not just being polite," Susan assured her.

"Of course, I know that."

That evening Deborah's mother called.

"So Ben and I have had a long talk and he tells me that he has spoken to you?" Brina said without emotion.

"Yes, we did speak over lunch. Are you okay?"

"Of course I'm okay. My life is almost over, and I no longer think very much about it. I pray that Ben won't suffer too much, that his sons will be as good to him as he's been to them, and that they'll understand our life together, but that too is doubtful."

"So, if they don't, then what?"

"If they don't, they don't. You know and I know that life goes on, and when it comes to the really important things, we have little control. Whatever God there is, if there is, must take great pleasure in watching us all make fools of ourselves."

"Mom, this doesn't sound like you."

"So, who should I sound like? I have no more tears and I'm too old for lust. I'm fine, really. My early years were good, then we had the terrible years, but since coming to America, it's hardly been bad at all. If it's over, it's over."

"But it's not your life that's coming to an end, it's Ben's, and maybe he can buy himself a few more good years anyway. It's happened with other people."

"Maybe, but part of becoming a mature adult is accepting the inevitable. If Ben dies, my life is over. I have no direction anymore. It's just over."

"Mom," Deborah begged, "stop it."

"No, you listen to me. I didn't kill myself in Treblinka and I'm not killing myself now. I will continue to eat, sleep, visit, talk, whatever, but life will still be over. I'm not young anymore and the fight in me is gone."

"And what about me and Carl and the kids? We're not important? You don't fight for us?"

"Of course you're important. There was a point when you were the most important, but thank God you're taken care of. So now, for me, Ben is the most important. Don't worry, I'm okay. I'll do what I have to do, and everything will be just fine."

"I love you, Mom."

"And I love you too, and I thank God for you every day, but there comes a time . . . I'm close to eighty . . . we have to face life differently. I've reached that time, that's all I'm saying. So you look good at those papers Ben gave you. What I don't need is more aggravation from a couple of spoiled brats, and things will be fine."

"You really think Ben's children will give you a hard time?"

"Do I think? Who knows? He has spoiled them so much that they never seem to have enough. Will they be happy? Of course not. What they'll do about it, that remains to be seen."

"Okay, whatever you say, Mom. I'll take as good of care of everything as I know how."

"Then that will be the very best care there is, of that I am sure."

Brina may have put her stoic face forward in speaking to Deborah, but Aunt Rose and Uncle Jake had no problem letting her know how worried and upset they were.

"This getting old is not good," Uncle Jake said to her on the first of many conversations concerning Ben's health. "It's not bad enough that we get old and die, but we also have to suffer the pain and indignity of a disease like cancer. Ben is a good man and he doesn't deserve to die like this. He should just kill himself before the real suffering begins."

"No one deserves to die like this, but why should he kill himself?" Aunt Rose remarked. "God doesn't have a place in heaven for people who decide to kill themselves."

Uncle Jake was annoyed, "And since when are you the expert on what God wants?" he asked.

Deborah sighed loudly, "This is not a good conversation. It's getting us nowhere. I think Ben needs everyone to be optimistic for him right now. If you behave like you think he's going to die, then he may stop fighting. Attitude is very important in dealing with a life-threatening disease. You have to be strong. Put a smile on your face and let Ben think that you are hopeful. Who knows? He may surprise us all."

Uncle Jake looked down. "I'm trying to hope, but I'm old and I'm tired and I think whatever hope I might have had as a young person got left behind in Germany."

"Jake," Aunt Rose sighed, "Don't talk like that. We've made a good life for ourselves here in America."

"Yes, of course we have, but without Ben, who knows what kind of life we would have made? The man was a gift from heaven, and look at how he is being repaid for all he's done."

"Stop it, both of you," Deborah said sternly. "There's a lot going on and somehow we have to put a smile on our faces and go forward. Maybe if we keep smiling, something good will happen that will keep us smiling."

Aunt Rose looked up, "Oy, always the optimist; from your mouth to God's ears," she said, looking at Deborah.

"Well, whatever you do, make sure that Ben doesn't see you this way—and it would really help my mother if you were strong for her as well."

Uncle Jake looked startled. "How can you say that to us? Haven't we always been there for your mother? When haven't we been strong for Brina?"

Deborah leaned forward and touched his shoulder. "I know, Uncle Jake; you and Aunt Rose have always been there for my mother and for me. We wouldn't have survived without you; and now she needs you to be strong again. Please don't let her see you so sad."

Aunt Rose interrupted, "We know how to behave ourselves. You know that. We cry on the inside and smile on the outside. That's what it means to be Jewish. It's a skill we have all acquired over the centuries."

"I knew I could count on you," Deborah said, kissing her on the cheek before she changed the subject.

February 1993

Deborah could never remember at any time in her life ever feeling depressed. The lessons that began back in Poland had remained with her throughout the years. *Act quickly, don't look back, push harder, and move forward, inch by inch, win or lose*. That was the mentality that guided her daily existence. For the first time that she could remember Deborah was consumed by a feeling of helplessness and there didn't seem to be anything she could do to make herself feel any better.

The impact of the Rabbi's murder became greater as the weeks went by. The synagogue had been her sanctuary, but everything about it was now laden with distrust. Each person who walked into the building was suspect. She couldn't think of anyone whom she would consider capable of murder, but someone was guilty, and if she couldn't figure out who it might be then that made her a very poor judge of character.

"That's ridiculous," Carl asserted with his usual confidence. "If the ability to commit a murder were an obvious trait, then there would be no unsolved murders."

"This is not the average murder, Carl—this was a Rabbi. Who could murder a Rabbi? This man represented God! Susan says it must have been a crime of great passion."

"Not everybody believes in God, and this Rabbi had become a very controversial man," Carl replied. "I know you haven't asked for my opinion, but I think what you're really upset about is Ben and your mother, and your mother's mortality. You don't want to deal with that, so you're focusing on the Rabbi." Carl held his hands in front of his face and ducked in an effort to lighten her mood.

"Maybe you're right," she answered, to his surprise. "I guess it's just everything all together. All of a sudden there are these situations that I have no control over. I can't stand it. I know you don't believe this but I think the Rabbi expected me to do something to avenge his death. That's why he appeared to me. I'm in a position to do something, Esther really isn't and that's why he came to me. I want to do something, and I can't do anything, that's what's so frustrating."

"But we don't have to sit by and do nothing. You've been reacting to events, rather than leading the way." Carl cleared his throat as he spoke. "That's not your style. You and I can snoop around the synagogue a lot more than we've been doing to see what we can uncover on our own, and we can also be a little more involved in preparing your mother for what's going on in her life. Even if we get nowhere, you'll probably feel better if you begin acting rather than reacting."

"Now, I'm impressed, *Doctor* Katzman. That's a lot of insight for a mere internist. You're right. I'm a control freak, and I can't sit by and let other people handle situations that I am so directly involved with. And even more than that, I can't bear to think that the day is coming when I will be burying my own mother. She's so much a part of me, there's no way I can survive without her."

"But that's what's so wonderful about life, Deb, that your mother's essence continues on in you, and in our own children as well. I'm not religious, and truly it's hard for me to believe that Rabbi Levinson really paid you a visit on his way to the afterlife, but that part of Jewish teaching always made great sense to me. Your father was a musician; he loved music. He passed the gift of music on to you and through you on to our own children. That gift is a very important part of our children's lives.

"Your relationship with your mother is a very unique one. You've shared a range of emotions with her that most people never experience, some happy and some perhaps better forgotten, but all of that remains with you."

Deborah threw her arms around Carl and squeezed tightly, "I don't think I ever loved you as much as I do right at this moment."

"Good, then let's go get some dinner. I want to quit while I'm ahead."

Despite Deborah's vague notion that everyone was capable of murder given the right set of circumstances, she and Carl drew up a short list of those people who were more capable than others. They decided to make a serious new start towards finding Rabbi Levinson's murderer. She did have many resources available to her through Susan King and even the staff in her own office that she had not been utilizing. All of this was about to change. Deborah brought the list she and Carl prepared to Detective Brody's office the following morning.

"Now, this is what I've been trying to get you to do for me all along!" he exclaimed.

"It took us some time to work through our grief," Deborah replied calmly, "but we would like to be more actively involved in this with you, because I, for one, don't think I can continue praying in a synagogue fearing that the person praying next to me murdered my Rabbi."

"I think if we begin worrying about what the person praying next to us is guilty of, coming to synagogue becomes much more complicated than necessary. Nevertheless, for whatever reason you're now on board, welcome. I need your help. My boss is all over me about this case. We've got to arrest someone."

"The right someone, I hope. Joyce Kaplan is afraid you'll arrest anyone just to get the case closed."

"I won't do that, but . . ."

"I don't even want to think about it," Deborah interrupted. "Let's go over these names a little more seriously."

"Okay. Let's see. Number one, you've got Leon Feldman. Why Leon Feldman?"

"This is a list of people who Carl and I think could be capable of murder. It doesn't necessarily mean that we think they did it. Leon Feldman, I believe, is a person with no moral convictions. In my opinion, he's capable of anything, depending on what's in it for him. He's abrasive and completely insensitive to what's going on around him. Frankly, though, there's no motive. If it wasn't for the Rabbi, Leon probably would have been fired years ago. There are people in this congregation who actually detest him."

"Why did the Rabbi want him here then? That doesn't make too much sense, does it?"

"I'm not sure. No one understood it completely. We thought the Rabbi was just being kind since he had been here so many years, or being 'Judaic' as they call it at Beth Torah."

"Is it possible there was some quid pro quo no one knew about?" Detective Brody asked.

"Who knows? Deborah shrugged. "If no one knew about it, then no one knew about it."

"Fair enough," he replied. "So, moving right along, the next name on your list is Simmy Monash."

"Again," Deborah explained, "we're talking about capable of murder. I don't know any reason why he might murder anybody, least of all Rabbi Levinson. There's just something very sinister about Simmy. A lot of us have felt that way, even without knowing about his porn money. Sometimes I think it's unfair, because he comes from a different culture than we are used to, and it just may be that we're not reading him appropriately."

"That's possible, too," Detective Brody agreed, "but whatever his culture is, we know he's not the least bit troubled about breaking the law as long as there's something in it for him."

"I've been thinking about that," Deborah answered, "and maybe we have to keep in mind that women are just a cheap commodity in the world that he comes from."

"My, my," Detective Brody smirked upon reading the next name on the list. "Esther Levinson! You believe the Rebbetzin is capable of murdering her husband?"

"I want to emphasize to you as emphatically as I can that Carl and I agree that she is strong enough to commit a murder. We know of no reason why she would have wanted to murder her husband."

"That's interesting. The Rabbi's mother is pretty sure her daughter-in-law did it, and she's working on figuring out how, but so far she's come up with nothing, and neither have we. Up till now I've thought it was just usual mother-in-law/daughter-in-law paranoia, but if you think there might be more to it, well, it's an interesting concept."

"I have no reason to think Esther is guilty. She most certainly was upset enough over his death and I don't even think the timeline works. I can't think of one reason why she would want to murder him. They always seemed to be very supportive of each other, but Leon says the Rabbi was calling her name before he died. Maybe he was trying to tell Leon who did it? Who do you think is the most likely suspect?"

"Number one on my list is Joyce Kaplan. She's got the motive and the guts to do it, but I don't have enough of a case to arrest her. I'm working on that."

"Detective, I can almost promise you that you're traveling on the wrong train. Joyce wouldn't consider getting her hands dirty in this fashion. There's nothing she likes better than leading a crusade and winning a good fight. She had become the Eleanor Roosevelt of Beth Torah. She had a whole group of people behind her and that will probably never happen again in her lifetime. Whoever murdered the Rabbi took the wind out of her sails. Joyce Kaplan was a selfish, over-indulged little girl who grew up to be a selfish, over-indulged woman, but she didn't have any reason to murder the Rabbi."

"He knew about her affair with Lester Calderon. You don't think that's enough of a reason? Matters of the heart can cause many a murder, I assure you."

"Absolutely, but it didn't cause this murder. It wouldn't destroy her marriage even if her husband found out about it—and he probably knows. Where else is Fred Kaplan going to go? He's got a good-looking wife and he works for her very rich father. On his own, he's nothing, so you think he's about to move out? Joyce needs instant gratification and Lester Calderon might have been her toy of the month. I am positive that this relationship represented nothing other than lust, an immediate thrill. I don't for one minute think there was love or passion involved on either side and, in my humble opinion, she didn't do it.

"The last name on my list is Rochelle Levy, the Sisterhood President. Again, she certainly seems like an illogical suspect, but unlike my husband, I see Rochelle as a strong woman who would do whatever she feels is necessary in any given situation. Rochelle stands up for herself all the time. Of course, I know of no reason why she would want to kill the Rabbi. She was, generally speaking, one of his defenders."

"And Barry?" Detective Brody asked. "Barry is not on your list?"

"Barry is a wimp," Deborah answered.

"So where does all this leave me?" Detective Brody sighed.

"At the beginning and pushing forward, full steam ahead," Deborah sighed.

March 1993

Another board of directors' meeting was approaching. Since the Rabbi's demise all board meetings had been very well attended. No one dared to fall behind on the latest rumors being circulated. Somehow news had been leaked about the Rabbi having some sort of ledger book, and that story had quickly developed further into the Rabbi having his own bookie.

"It would be a real *shanda* if that actually turned out to be true," said Joan Fishman, an attractive redhead. Joan was an interior decorator and she was in charge of Beth Torah's Refurbishing Committee. "Can you imagine if it turned out that he was killed because he owed somebody who knows how much money in gambling debts?"

"Listen to you," Simmy shouted, shaking his fist in the air. "Do you know what you're doing? You are profaning the name of a pious man: our Rabbi. Stop it. It's a terrible thing that you're doing."

"Come on, Simmy, everyone has some monkey that they're carrying around on their back. No one is perfect. Maybe the Rabbi really had a gambling problem. Who knows?" said Arnold Wexler, a stockbroker who was currently assisting the treasurer in investing the synagogue's endowment fund money. Arnold winked at Deborah as he spoke. He enjoyed getting Simmy all riled up just so he could watch his reaction. "The best side show in town," he had been heard to say.

"This is not a monkey we're talking about," Simmy bellowed even louder, unwittingly playing the game by Arnold's rules. "This is a Rabbi, our Rabbi. Have some respect," Once again he reached into his pocket for the crumpled handkerchief to wipe his eyes. "I can't believe what you would do to his memory."

"Enough already, Arnold," said Rochelle in a stern voice. "Simmy is right. This is our Rabbi we're talking about, and we all knew him well enough to know that he was no gambler. I don't know who started this rumor, but it is ridiculous and let's all stop it already."

As Rochelle spoke, Deborah realized that Harry was not at her side.

"How's Harry doing?" she asked.

"A little under the weather today, but he'll be fine," Rochelle responded.

"I think," said Deborah, "that we all have to try very hard to separate some of the ridiculous stories going around from the truth. We should work together to find out who the murderer is and get this heinous crime resolved so that we can move forward as a synagogue family.

"Whether we want to admit it or not, it is very possible that one of us sitting here at this table is a murderer. Look at the person sitting next to you, and start to think carefully about anything you might know that could prove helpful in solving the murder. I don't mean to make anyone paranoid, but don't consider that you're being loyal to a friend by not passing on important information, because if you are holding back anything that might be helpful, you could inadvertently be making it more difficult for us to find the person who killed our Rabbi."

Joyce Kaplan called Deborah at home the day after the board meeting.

"Do you know if I am still a suspect in this case?" she asked bluntly. "No one's been around to see me lately."

"I believe we're all suspects at the moment," Deborah replied.

"Oh, come on. I can get that bullshit from Detective Brody. I see the way things are going, and that Detective is snooping all over the place. Do you know if I'm a suspect?"

"I think you are one of several suspects, but I assure you there's no real evidence linking you to the crime that I know of." Deborah understood her concern, and she was quite certain that Joyce was not the murderer.

"Of course not. If there was, that Detective What's His Face would have arrested me already. How do you like this fucking Rabbi? Even in death he's plaguing me."

"I wish you wouldn't talk like that to me, Joyce. I find it hard to deal with. I may not have agreed with everything the Rabbi was doing, but I did have respect for Rabbi Levinson's convictions, and I certainly feel we should have reverence for him in death."

"Yeah, you're right," Joyce replied calmly, to Deborah's surprise. "It's just that I'm really frustrated and I have no way to let it all out."

"I know. I'm feeling that way too," Deborah responded. "Why don't you help me find the real murderer, then we can deal with all of this frustration in a positive manner?"

"Oh, sure, let me go rub my crystal ball and I'll call you right back. Actually, if you want to know the truth, I think it's either Simmy or Leon myself."

"Why do you say that? Do you know something?" Deborah asked, sounding suddenly very animated.

"No, I don't know anything. It's just that they're the two people around the synagogue who would get my vote as the 'Most Likely to Kill a Rabbi.'"

"Simmy always loved the Rabbi and he is still protecting him," Deborah said, playing devil's advocate.

"Never trust anyone who protests too much. My father always says that about business deals. Simmy is just crying too loudly. Simmy Monash is a sneaky little bastard. I can't think of why, in particular, he would murder the Rabbi, but I don't trust him."

"See," Deborah responded, "that's the problem. No one can come up with a good motive."

"You mean Detective Brody doesn't think my little rendezvous with Les Calderon is a motive for murder?"

"Yes, it's a motive, but not a real strong one that will hold up without any hard evidence. I think you're safe."

"Well, that's a relief," said Joyce with a deep sigh. "And, incidentally, I don't know if this means anything, and I don't know if the story is even true, but Leon is the one who leaked that bit about the ledger book the Rabbi was keeping."

"Are you sure about that?" Deborah asked.

"Of course I'm sure. I'm one of the people he leaked it to."

"You are? What did he say?"

"Just that he heard the Rabbi was keeping a ledger book, and that that might be a motive for the killing, but the police hadn't yet figured out what the ledger book was keeping track of and they couldn't tie it to the murder."

"How did he come to tell you this, Joyce?" Deborah asked, suddenly taking a more serious posture.

"No reason. We were just talking about who it could have been, and he volunteered that information."

"That's interesting. Well, if it's any consolation to you, I think you can relax," Deborah assured her. "Let's keep in touch and try to get on top of any clue that comes along."

"Sounds good."

"Bye."

Chapter Nineteen

February 1993

Deborah left a message for Detective Brody to stop by her office the next morning, she was very anxious to speak to him. When he arrived, Deborah's secretary directed him to the library, where she was preparing the opening statement for an upcoming trial that was about to begin.

"I'm glad to see you," she sais, smiling. "Please sit down."

"I'm hoping you have some real information for me," he responded. "It's about time I had a break in this case."

"Maybe. I think I may have picked up a helpful tidbit." Deborah couldn't help but be amused watching Detective Brody hang on her every word. She continued, "Did you ever speak to Leon about the ledger book you found?"

"No, I sure didn't. I'm still trying to figure out what it's for. The only ones I've mentioned the ledger book to are you and the good doctor."

"Apparently Leon Feldman knows about it."

"Not from me he doesn't," Detective Brody said.

"Not from us either, but he leaked information concerning the existence of the ledger book to at least one congregant I know of and possibly more. And there is now a lot of speculation and gossiping going around about what exactly the ledger book was for."

"Okay, counselor, you tell me: What do you make of all of that?"

The detective's body language changed abruptly. He sat upright, placing his hands on top of the table in front of him. He was focused on her every word, and as she spoke the creases in his forehead became more pronounced.

"Carl and I discussed it last night. If no one told him about the ledger book and he knows about it, then it's reasonable to assume he has something to do with it. It's even possible that by beginning a rumor he was hoping to deflect attention away from himself."

"I'm impressed. Good deduction. So, let's see if we can take this a little bit further. What could all of this have to do with the Rabbi's murder?"

"I'm not sure. Maybe Leon owed the Rabbi some money and the ledger book is a record of payment."

"Do you think the Rabbi earned enough money to be lending large sums to your administrator? If that's the case every Rabbi in the country must be applying for this job!"

"Okay, so maybe it wasn't the Rabbi who lent him the money, maybe someone else lent him money and the Rabbi was just being a nice guy and keeping track of the payment schedule." That sounded absurd as she spoke the words, even to her own ears. "I guess that is also ridiculous. The Rabbi would never get involved in something like that. But what I can't understand is why Leon didn't take the ledger book out of the office before you could find it. That's what doesn't make sense."

"Aha," Detective Brody said smugly, "now, we're getting somewhere. Maybe he couldn't find the ledger book. It was well hidden. If the trained crew we sent in hadn't gone through every inch of the Rabbi's office we never would have found it."

Deborah suddenly remembered how upset Leon had been when the Acting Rabbi arrived early. "That makes sense. He didn't even want to let Rabbi Klein into the office when he got here. He locked him out."

"Right, and he must have assumed that the police would find the ledger eventually and perhaps link it up to him, so he tried to push suspicion elsewhere." Detective Brody was so visibly excited he literally jumped for joy. "In my spare time I do jigsaw puzzles. My wife thinks I'm crazy. She says it's a waste of time, but I love putting all the pieces together. I start with fifteen hundred individual pieces of cardboard, and I work on it, developing it piece by piece, one layer at a time, until it's completed." His voice was bursting with excitement. "This is the interesting part of the job, putting all the pieces of the puzzle together. This is great."

"I'm glad you're so happy. But I'm not sure of what it all means," Deborah persisted. "Let's assume the ledger book does have something to do with Leon. We can even assume that Leon was paying money to the Rabbi for some crazy, unknown reason. But what next? And how does that connect him to the murder?"

"We don't know yet, but now we can move on to the next layer of the puzzle. We go back and look at the figures in the book a little differently. If we start with the assumption that it's Leon who's paying money for something, maybe it will begin to fit together. I'll get back to you."

"Thank you, and you can let yourself out. I'm working on my opening statement for a trial that's starting tomorrow."

The evening newspaper headline read: "New Evidence in Rabbi's Murder, Arrest Imminent."

"You don't have to keep picking me up at the hospital," Deborah's mother insisted. "The bus stops right at the corner."

"I don't have to do anything I don't want to do," said Deborah, gently touching her mother's hand.

"Ben does seem to be responding to treatment. I didn't expect it, but he is. And that doctor is very nice to us since Carl called him."

"I'm sure he would have been nice to you under any circumstances. He's trained to deal with people who are suffering."

"Take my word for it," her mother replied very matter-of-factly, "The doctor was always pleasant, but there was a difference after he spoke to Carl. We're no longer just a room number on the third floor; now, at least, he remembers our names. And it was good that Ben's children could see that too, that someone I know could be making a difference for the better. It helped with my having to be with them so often. It is all very awkward."

"So his children are spending a lot of time with you at the hospital?"

"Actually, now they do. In the beginning, they didn't. But Ben goes for chemo every other week, and it's hard because he's so sick afterwards. And each time seems to get worse instead of better. We all feel we have to be there for him. Maybe it's just an act for Ben's sake, but they are very civil to me."

"If they have any intelligence at all and any love for Ben, they have to realize that he needed a normal life of some sort. You provided that for him, Mom, and they should be grateful."

"Grateful? Grateful, you think they should be? That's something." Brina laughed. "I just hope he told them about the money. In my experience everything is wonderful until we start dividing up money. But in the meantime, Ben is responding well to the chemo, and God willing we have a little time until we have to handle financial matters."

"I love you, Mom, and I thank you for everything you gave to me."

"Stop it, or we'll both be crying in a few minutes. We don't need this. We both know what we went through and what we did for each other. Other people may not understand, but you and I? We understand. It doesn't have to be spoken. We know what it is. Our bones ache from the twisting and turning we did for each other. But it's over, and we've moved on. You're a wonderful daughter and I'm proud of you. You have a wonderful husband, wonderful children, and a wonderful career. Now, let's change the subject."

Deborah smiled. "Okay, I know enough to quit while we're ahead."

April 1993

Deborah saw Esther Levinson regularly at synagogue. Esther came each morning to say *Kaddish*, although as a woman she was still not counted in the *minyan* at Beth Torah. Dr. Levinson and his wife Sonia also came to say *Kaddish* each morning for their son. Rabbi Klein didn't think he should change the Temple's practice since he was only there for a short while. Apart from what Detective Brody had told her, Deborah had herself sensed some tension between the two women in Rabbi Levinson's life, although they were each very careful to be cordial to each other for the sake of appearances. Deborah did not want to believe that Esther Levinson would have killed her husband for whatever reason, and she chose to put all such thoughts completely out of her mind.

Deborah had started coming to the morning *minyan* whenever possible shortly after Brian and Seth moved out of the house. She had decided to say *Kaddish* every morning for the family and friends whose lives were lost at the hands of the Nazis. She didn't know the date of her father's death, and every day, for sure, many people had died who have no one to say *Kaddish* for them.

One morning when she was in less of a rush than usual, Deborah asked Esther if she would care to have breakfast with her.

Esther hesitated for a moment before answering. "I have to be in the city by ten, but if we don't take too long I think that might be nice."

They drove to the local bagel store.

"How are you getting along by yourself?" Deborah had extended the invitation on a whim, and found herself groping for conversation.

"It's getting better. I've had a little time now to reflect on our lives together. In many ways Saul and I were more dependent on each other than most people would have thought. We had no children, you know."

"Of course," Deborah responded. "And you were both so involved with children in your jobs."

"Yes, that's true," Esther agreed, offering no further information on the subject.

"I remember a number of years ago, when my children were at a Zionist camp for the summer, I was going to bring them home early because they kept calling to complain about the food. I was afraid they might starve to death or some such thing over the summer. I went to see Rabbi Levinson to talk to him about the problem, and he told me I had to learn to make a distinction between food for the soul and food for the body. He assured me that my children could eat food for the body every day of the year, but during this very short period of time they were living Judaism in a way that would not be possible in the secular world, and it was here that their souls were being fed."

Esther smiled. "That certainly sounds like Saul. He had a very mystical quality about him."

"Yes," Deborah agreed. "He also promised me that my children would not come home suffering from malnutrition." They both laughed. "You must miss him very much," Deborah said softly.

"Yes, I do, of course. But, as you know, he had become more and more inflexible over the years, and to be honest, he had become quite difficult to live with."

"I understand that, too," Deborah assured her.

"Yes, I know you do. It's astonishing to me, but reflecting on our life together I can remember back to Saul's first congregation at a small synagogue in upstate New York. We thought we were miserable there and couldn't wait for his contract to run out, but now, in retrospect, those were among the best years of our marriage, because we were working together as a team. We had a common goal, which somehow disappeared over time. In some ways we had a good marriage. I never questioned Saul's love and devotion—we did love each other—but in spite of all that, as the years went by, we began to lead separate lives."

Deborah had not expected Esther to be so candid with her. "You mentioned that he had become difficult. Why do you think that happened?"

"I don't have an easy answer to that; a lot of different reasons, probably. He was very close to his grandfather and often called him for advice. His grandfather was a very educated man, but his mentality was that of a *shtetl* Jew. That doesn't work very well in a sophisticated Jewish community. In the early years his grandfather was not the only influence on Saul, but as time went on Saul listened more and more to the old man and less to me and others around him, and when his grandfather died I believe Saul felt the need to adhere totally to his grandfather's brand of Judaism. He used to tell me the old man came to speak to him in his dreams. I think he honestly believed that was real."

Oh my God, Deborah thought. She could feel the goose bumps crawling up her body. Rabbi Levinson's grandfather appeared to him in dreams, and now the Rabbi himself had appeared to her in her dream. If the Rabbi was accustomed to communicating in this way, maybe it wasn't so strange that he came to her. Maybe it was her own fear that didn't allow her to hear what he had to say. She suddenly realized that Esther seemed to be waiting for her to speak. Deborah took a deep breath, "Esther, who do you think killed the Rabbi?"

"I have no idea. Saul unfortunately made so many enemies within the last few years. Of course, I wouldn't have thought any of them would have murdered him."

"Have you noticed anyone behaving strangely since the Rabbi's death?"

Esther thought a minute and then laughed, "Everyone's behavior has been very strange since Saul died. Simmy never stops crying. Barry never seems to know what to say. Rochelle has stopped talking altogether. People see me on the street and they cross over to the other side, and if they have no way to avoid me, and they are forced to say 'Hello,' they immediately begin to stutter. No one knows how to behave with me so everyone has been behaving oddly."

Deborah nodded her understanding.

"Also, Deborah, although you have been kind enough not to say anything to me yet, I want to assure you that I will be out of the house by the end of the summer."

Deborah was overjoyed to hear that. "Please take as much time as you need. I don't want to be pushing you out of your home."

"No, it's fine, I'm actually anxious to move. I've begun looking for an apartment in Manhattan and I'm sure I will be out by the end of August. I appreciate your consideration."

"I'm glad I had this opportunity to speak with you."

"Yes," Esther agreed. "Perhaps we can get together another time."

Detective Brody sounded very excited when he called to make certain that Deborah would be able to see him. She agreed to meet him at the synagogue. It was Leon Feldman's day off and they were able to talk in his office. Deborah had asked the bookkeeper to give her a list of the various funds that the synagogue maintained.

"I wanted to meet you here so we could go over these funds together," Detective Brody told her.

"Well, I have a list of the synagogue funds."

"Which of those funds would someone be able to get into without being noticed?" Detective Brody asked.

"You think Leon was stealing money from the synagogue?"

"That's a real possibility, and he is, of course, a likely candidate at the moment. But even leaving personalities out of this for the time being and just concentrating on these funds, how often are they looked at and how are they invested?"

"The treasurer has a committee that decides how to invest the funds. It's made up of mostly investment bankers who are also congregants and accountants. I'm not that involved with this, but I do believe that the money is invested very conservatively in municipal bonds, CDs, that type of stuff."

"Is any of it left in a savings account?"

"Sure. But we need two signatures to withdraw money from our savings account. Leon is one of the two signatures that could be used, along with one of the Temple officers."

"So if he had someone else willing to go along with him, or if he were good at forging a signature, he could be withdrawing money: right or wrong?"

"Wrong, I think. I would like to believe that the treasurer is asking for an accounting of money that is being withdrawn. Rochelle has been treasurer for six out of the last ten years, and I know she's always been very careful about accounting for every *shekel*. I don't believe money could be easily withdrawn from one of Beth Torah's bank accounts. although, obviously, we can get an accounting of what has been taken out."

"Obviously," said Detective Brody. "How about just pocketing money that comes in for one of the funds? Is it possible, do you think, that the money never makes it to the bank?"

"Generally, checks are made out to the synagogue because that's a tax deduction. If someone is deducting money for tax purposes, and the checks are not making it into one of the synagogue's bank accounts, I think that also is a somewhat unlikely occurrence."

"Yes, well, we need these fund accounts gone over by an auditor, a forensic accountant maybe, with a fine-tooth comb, to see if anything is missing. Maybe someone has a friend at the bank. Who knows? Anything is possible."

"I believe that between the bookkeeper and the treasurer we should be able to account for all of the money that's been taken in by the synagogue. Auditors are really expensive and I don't think it's in Beth Torah's budget right now."

Deborah pulled out a scratch pad and made a note to herself.

"Also," Detective Brody added, "maybe we can figure out where the Rabbi was putting the money he was collecting and keeping track of in the ledger book."

"Sounds like a good place to start to me. If you give me a list of the dates where entries were made in the ledger, I'll bring the synagogue's books over to my own office. I've got a good friend who has a criminal law practice. She has trained forensic accountants on staff who can look these things over for us."

"Actually, we should do it at the police station."

"No. If you don't mind, I'd rather keep it at my office. That way I know I'll get the books back where they belong very quickly."

Detective Brody grinned. "You don't trust me to get the books back quickly?"

"I think I'd just rather do it myself." Deborah didn't know why, but somehow she felt better about not having the police nosing their way through the synagogue's private records. "Maybe I don't want how our synagogue spends money to be the topic of conversation around some police bar. This is our business, so let me see if I can take care of it."

"Touchy, touchy, but okay. I have to warn you though, if you don't find anything it doesn't mean that we won't look after you're done."

"Fair enough. But if there's anything to find, I'm certain that Susan King's investigators will find it. They're very sharp."

"Susan King, the criminal attorney, is your friend?" Detective Brody was obviously surprised.

"Yes, for many years. Does that bother you?" Deborah was sounding a bit hostile.

"Oh, no," he quickly replied. "It's just that given her reputation I would have to say that you're not very much alike."

"That's true in some ways and untrue in others, but under any circumstances we have a long history together and we are very close friends."

Susan arrived at Deborah's office at six o'clock in the evening, laden with sandwiches and soda. At Deborah's request Susan had brought her chief forensic accountant with her, a woman named Laney Baer. Deborah knew Laney by reputation and knew that she had become Susan's right arm in preparing cases for trial. "Couldn't have done it without her," Deborah had heard Susan say often. Laney had learned to decipher some very convoluted bookkeeping systems.

"Don't worry, Deborah," Susan assured her. "If there is anything to be found, Laney will find it."

Deborah had hoped things would fall into place like they do on all those television detective programs, that a clever but glaring scheme would leap out at Laney from this hodgepodge of numbers, and Laney would stand up and shout, "By golly, I've found it!" And then they would immediately telephone Detective Brody who would run out with his gun and handcuffs and arrest someone.

It was nine o'clock when Carl, looking very glum, stopped by the office to see her. Laney had still not found anything. Carl greeted Susan warmly, but Deborah could tell instantly from his manner that something was wrong. He motioned her into another room.

"I have some sad news," he said in a somber tone. "Rochelle's son died. She is trying to keep this as a private matter, but I thought you should know."

Deborah was astounded. "Don't tell me he was murdered too?"

"My God, no," Carl responded, shocked. "Her son Jonathan died of AIDS early this evening. He had been hospitalized for many months at Beth Israel in Manhattan. But when he decided to go off all medication, he came back to Long Island and Rochelle asked me to work with his doctor in Manhattan and handle his case on an as-needed basis in emergency situations. I signed the death certificate this evening."

"Why didn't you ever mention this to me?" Deborah was upset at the news, but was also irate to be hearing about it in this way.

Carl had prepared himself for this type of response. He and Deborah rarely kept secrets from each other. "I'm sorry. Maybe I should have said something sooner, but Rochelle specifically asked me not to tell you or anyone else, and I felt I had to respect her wishes. I'm sure she still doesn't want anyone to know." Carl looked down to avoid eye contact.

"Why not? Why doesn't she want anyone to know?" Deborah asked, her tone of voice clearly conveying her anger.

"You can't be that naive, Deborah. She's ashamed. AIDS is hard on everyone, but women like Rochelle are among the least well equipped to handle it."

"So why tell me now?"

"Because I think maybe she needs someone to talk to. They're having a graveside burial for him tomorrow morning. She doesn't even know if her husband will attend. Harry never forgave his son for his lifestyle and certainly never forgave him for getting sick. I don't know. I just feel sorry for her. I think she needs a shoulder to cry on."

"I don't like that you didn't trust me enough to tell me about this before her son died. I know that I would have confided in you if I were in your place. What I'm feeling is that I would like you to get out and leave me alone. On the chance that you're right and she does need someone to talk to, I wouldn't want to let her down, so I'll go to the cemetery in the morning, but right now, I'd like you to leave."

Carl nodded. "We'll talk later." He touched her shoulder and left.

"What's the matter?" Susan asked, recognizing that Deborah's demeanor had changed completely.

"A friend's son has died of AIDS," Deborah explained. "Carl's been treating him, but he never told me anything about it until this very minute."

"And that makes you angry?" Susan asked.

"Very. I thought we had no secrets from each other. But our friend didn't want anyone to know, so he didn't tell me."

"Carl is right. He's a doctor. He has to respect that kind of request, particularly where AIDS is involved. You can't imagine how devastating a disease it is unless you've lived with it." Obviously, Susan had known people who lived with it.

Deborah sighed. "Why don't we call it a night."

"Yes. Laney can come into your office in the morning. You don't have to be here for her to continue working on the books," Susan suggested.

"Are you sure you can spare her?"

"No, I can't, but I will. It shouldn't take much longer. Go speak to your friend. She needs you."

Chapter Twenty

April 1993

Deborah drove towards Rochelle's house. If she saw lights on, she would ring the bell; if the house were dark, she would wait until the morning and call her early. She couldn't remember what time Carl had said the funeral was, or if he had said. Harry Levy was an investment broker, and apparently a very successful one, judging from the Levy family's lifestyle. In addition to being a very caring husband, Harry had also been very generous to everyone in his family, and most especially to Rochelle over the years. Rochelle requested little for herself personally, but she loved buying nice things for their home. Their collection of impressionist art was museum quality, and the envy of everyone who had occasion to view it. Rochelle and Harry regularly examined the newspapers in search of interesting auctions. Their home was in an estate area with two-acre zoning. It was a traditional colonial-style house, well built and sturdy, with large comfortable rooms, but not particularly opulent. In keeping with Rochelle's rather simple style of living, other than the magnificent paintings that adorned the walls, the house was decidedly understated.

The Levys' house was located one block off the main road, and driving by Deborah could see lights on in both the front and back of the house, so she drove up the circular driveway, and parked under the overhang that led to the front door.

Rochelle answered the knock on the door, her face was swollen from crying.

"Oh, Rochelle, I'm so sorry," said Deborah, throwing her arms around her and hugging her tightly.

Rochelle immediately began sobbing. "It's so terrible. You can't imagine how terrible it is."

"How long has he been sick?" Deborah asked.

"Two years, maybe three. Who knows? It seems like forever. He was such a caring, wonderful person. I don't know how this could happen."

"Are you alone?"

"Harry's upstairs, but we're hardly talking to each other. My daughter Laura is flying in tonight on the red-eye from California for the funeral."

Rochelle and Harry were so close, it was hard to envision them not speaking to each other. "When was the last time Laura saw Jonny?"

"She hasn't seen him for at least four or five months. He didn't want her to come. He didn't want her to see him like he was. You just can't imagine, Deborah, how terrible it is. He couldn't eat, he's been on intravenous feedings for almost a year. He was a shadow of himself, a walking skeleton. For the last two months all he did was cry. He didn't want to die. He was afraid. I would go into that hospital ward and see all those beautiful young men with so much to live for, and they were all dying. It's just so awful."

"I wish you would have told me, Rochelle. I would have tried to help you while Jonny was alive," Deborah was straining to find the right thing to say.

"I couldn't bear to live with people knowing my son had AIDS. Maybe I'm a coward, but I saw what went on in the hospital with other families, and I decided not to tell anyone. You become a pariah. People you thought were friends are afraid to go near you. Harry, my own husband, Jonny's father, was afraid to go near him. He never went to the hospital. He never forgave Jonny for being gay, and he never forgave him for getting sick. But Harry's upstairs crying now, and I can't even speak to him."

"Tell me, Rochelle, did you ever speak to Rabbi Levinson about Jonny?" Deborah asked, remembering what the Rabbi had written in his diary.

Rochelle looked down at the floor, tears still streaming down her cheeks. "I couldn't tell anybody, I was afraid. And how could I tell Rabbi Levinson? You know what the Bible says about homosexuality. Rabbi Levinson would never have been understanding. I was ashamed for what Jonny was, and I'm ashamed because I felt ashamed. Does that make any sense?"

"Of course it does," Deborah spoke softly, "but you needn't feel ashamed. Jonny was a good boy and a part of him lives on in you and the other people whose lives he touched. There's nothing to be ashamed of,"

Deborah said, realizing that she was mouthing sentiments recently expressed by Carl. Deborah also wondered how Rabbi Levinson would have known about Jonny being gay if Rochelle didn't tell him. Maybe it was Leon.

"You can't imagine how people react to you. You don't understand, because you haven't lived through it. But it's over, and at least my poor baby won't have to suffer anymore."

"You look tired, Rochelle. Why don't you try to get some rest? Maybe you and Harry can talk about this in a few days, after the funeral, to try and work things out. You've always had such a caring relationship, and you really need each other right now. I'll see you in the morning. Carl and I are coming to the cemetery."

"There's nothing I can say to Harry. He won't talk to me or anyone. I don't know if he's feeling guilty or what, but I can't speak to him. The last month has not been easy. I'm waiting up for Laura. She's taking a taxi from the airport. Deborah, please, promise me you won't talk about this in the synagogue."

Deborah squeezed her hand. "Don't worry, 'Our Gang' won't hear a sound from me. But I believe you would get much more support than you think."

Carl was reading in bed when Deborah arrived home. "I stopped by to see Rochelle, she's pretty upset."

"Yes, of course. Are you still angry at me?"

"Yes, but I guess I understand why you felt you had to do what you did."

"I wanted to tell you. I almost did more than once, but I felt I had to respect Rochelle's privacy. This has been a terrible ordeal for all of them. Harry never came to terms with it. I'm glad you understand."

"I wouldn't go that far. You see, I thought we trusted each other and I felt secure, confident that what we had transcended anything else that might happen around us. I'm sad for Rochelle and poor Jonny and even for Harry, who probably will never have another peaceful day in his life, and maybe I shouldn't be saying this in the same breath as talking about a young man dying and parents losing their son, but I also feel like I lost something tonight, because the wall of confidence that made me feel so secure has been chipped, and that makes me sad."

"I'm sorry," Carl said softly, knowing there was nothing left to say.

The graveside service for Jonathan Levy was attended by Rochelle and her daughter Laura. Harry decided to come after all, but he stood quietly in the background as though he were a passerby at a stranger's grave. There were several people whom Deborah didn't recognize, probably relatives. Deborah and Carl were the only nonfamily members present. A young female Rabbi had been visiting Jonny daily in the hospital; she was the one Rochelle contacted to conduct the brief service.

Deborah approached Harry. "I'm sorry," she said.

"So am I," he answered. "I don't know why he turned out the way he did and I don't understand why he had to die. At least a son of mine should have been smart enough to be careful."

"Jonny was a wonderful young man, and you raised him well. He got sick and died. He couldn't help that."

"Maybe yes, maybe no," Harry answered, sounding like a man in great distress. "If I believed in God I'd think that maybe he's found some peace, but I know better."

"Harry, you don't believe in God?" Deborah responded. "I can't believe that. You're so involved with the Temple."

"So what has that got to do with believing in God? If there was a God, do you think my son would have died like this? There's no God, Deborah, I assure you. You, of all people, with what you've been through in your lifetime, you should know that."

Deborah decided this was not the moment to have a philosophical conversation with Harry Levy.

The family was gathering back at the Levy house, but Deborah did not feel comfortable doing that. No mention had been made of sitting *shiva*, and Deborah wondered what they were doing, but she and Carl had come in separate cars and they each went on to do what they had to do. However, Rabbi Levinson was buried in the same cemetery, and before leaving Deborah drove her car over to his grave. The headstone had not yet been put in place.

"God," she mumbled. "I never knew anyone who was buried in this cemetery and now I've been to two funerals under shocking circumstances within a short time. Life is filled with surprises."

Deborah stood in front of Rabbi Levinson's grave staring at the mound of earth in front of her. It had stopped raining, and a fog or a mist appeared to be moving in above the grave site. The air around her once again felt heavy. Her heart was pounding. The skin on her arms and legs began to tingle. A gust of wind rushed past her with a bit of a whistle, and in that moment Deborah was sure that she heard someone whisper her name. She looked towards the road, but no one was in sight.

"Oh, God, I'm losing my mind," she cried out loud. "I've got to get out of here."

She began to walk towards the car, at first slowly but gradually faster and faster, her heart still pounding. Once safely in her car she looked back at the rows of gravestones and bushes she had just passed. Did Rabbi Levinson come to speak to her or was her imagination on overdrive?

Deborah floored the gas pedal, the wheels screeched, and she drove off faster than anyone should be driving in a cemetery.

Chapter Twenty-One

April 1993

There was a frantic message from Leon awaiting her at the office. She returned his call promptly.

"Where have you been?" Leon asked. "We've been looking all over for you."

"I was attending a funeral, Leon. I'm sorry if I can't give you a twenty-four-hour accounting of my time," Deborah said, her voice dripping with sarcasm.

"You were at Rochelle's son's funeral?" Leon asked.

"I didn't know you knew about it," Deborah answered.

"There's very little I don't know about around here," he said with assurance.

"Okay, then, what's the problem?" she asked.

"The problem is canaries."

"Canaries?"

"Yeah, canaries. This may sound ludicrous, but there is something you have to handle. There's more to being president than searching for murderers, you know."

"I can hardly wait to hear what comes next."

"Rita Calderon's son is having his Bar Mitzvah this weekend. They're having a huge party on Saturday night in the ballroom and Rita is apparently using canaries as part of the centerpiece on each of the tables."

"That sounds a bit ridiculous, but so what?"

"So, the caterer is having fits. He says it's unsanitary and he can't have canaries sitting in the middle of his food."

"So let him explain this to Rita and Lester. What does it have to do with us?"

"Rita insists that she's promised each of her son's friends that they would receive a canary in a cage before they go home."

"That's a novel idea. I thought it was the guests who brought the presents. When did this change come about?"

"Listen, Deborah, you are not taking this seriously enough. The caterer says that he can't speak to Rita or Lester again. They won't listen to anything he has to say, and if the canaries are sitting on the tables, he is leaving without serving any food. He will not take a chance on someone getting sick and suing him. He has written me a letter to that effect. He's right. You're a lawyer, you know how people sue over nothing these days."

"I understand what you are saying, Leon. What I don't understand is why this is our problem. If the caterer doesn't serve any food, that becomes Rita and Lester's problem, not ours."

"The arithmetic is quite elementary," Leon said, making no attempt to hide his exasperation. "In the realm of how things happen, this becomes an administration problem. As you know, the synagogue depends heavily on a percentage of the caterer's profits that he turns over to us. Without that money we'd never make our budget every year. It's too late for the Calderons to go somewhere else with their canaries, and if the caterer doesn't serve the food, Rita will tell everyone what happened, and no one in the YCC group will want to use the caterer, so his business will be cut down to nothing, we will stop getting profits from his parties and we will be off budget by maybe fifty to seventy-five thousand next year. So now do you understand why this is our problem?"

"Only if I accept everything you say as true. I have no interest in this at all, Leon. Our Rabbi was murdered, remember? I just went to the funeral of a friend's son. I have no interest in getting involved in this trivial crap."

"You're the president. This is your responsibility. I've done about as much as I can. It's up to you at this point."

"I will go as far as one phone call to Rita, but I promise you that is all I am going to do."

"Bless you. Call and let me know what happens."

"But of course."

◆

Deborah went to look up Rita's phone number. *What a day.* She wondered if someone like Rita could even begin to comprehend the tragedy of having a child die of AIDS.

"Hello," Rita said slowly and seductively, upon answering the phone.

"Hello, Rita. This is Deborah Katzman, and I hear you're crazy about canaries." Deborah was attempting to make light of what she knew had to be one of the most absurd scenarios she would ever be asked to handle.

Rita laughed. "I really do love canaries. I love to hear them sing. I thought it would be nice for each of the children to have a party favor that would last a long time. This way every time they hear their canary sing, they'll keep remembering how much fun they had at my son's Bar Mitzvah."

"Oh, I think the idea is a wonderful one, believe me Rita, and I understand where you're coming from. But the caterer is just afraid that it's a little bit unsanitary to have birds sitting in the middle of all the food."

"Lester and I have discussed it, and we have decided that our centerpieces are none of his business. It's our money."

Deborah realized that she had to change tactics. "Actually, Rita, it's probably not too healthy for the canaries either. I mean, you know how kids are. If only one child gives some people food to one of these birds and the bird becomes sick and dies on the spot, that would really put a damper on the party, don't you think? I mean, do you know whether or not canaries can digest chopped herring?"

"God, you're right. I never thought about that. But I've promised them all a canary. Now I don't know what to do. This is terrible!"

"Well, maybe we could just keep the canaries in one of the classrooms of the religious school, and at the end of the party you can bring the children into that room and they can each pick out their own bird. How does that sound for an idea?"

"Oh my God, Deborah, you're brilliant. No wonder they made you the first woman president. Thank you. I'd better call the florist though. They've been working on decorating the bird cages, but now I need a totally different centerpiece. There's so little time. This is crazy, they'll never get it all done."

"Oh, somehow I'm sure you'll think of something very unique and beautiful, Rita. I'm not worried about you. And *mazel tov*, I hope you have a wonderful party."

"Thank you."

Deborah hung up and called Leon to explain how it all would be handled.

"You're a genius," Leon proclaimed, upon hearing the new game plan.

"In this lifetime, Leon, we all learn to handle whatever it is we have to handle. For one person it's the death of a child, for another it's canaries. It may be unfair, but that's just the way it is. The problem eventually passes, and then life goes on."

"Such a prophet; you and Isaiah. I'm really impressed."

"No, Leon, it's me and my namesake. I'm named for Deborah, who was a Judge, and I'm now a lawyer. We women have few enough biblical role models, let's at least give us the credit we deserve."

That evening Carl was called in on an emergency at the hospital. Deborah was alone in bed thinking of Rabbi Levinson.

"Rabbi," she said, barely whispering, "I'm trying, but I don't know what to do next. Was it you who was trying to speak to me at the cemetery, Rabbi? If you are out there and you can hear me, please send me a sign, an idea, anything." Deborah waited, but nothing happened and she fell asleep wondering if the Rabbi was still able to make earthly contact. Perhaps he had passed on to *Gan Eden* and had left her to finish the job of finding his murderer all on her own. Perhaps Carl was right and everything that happened was a figment of her overactive imagination. "Help me Rabbi, I need help," she whispered again, right before drifting off to sleep.

Chapter Twenty-Two

April 1993

L aney Baer spent several days studying the synagogue funds again and again, but could uncover nothing suspicious. Deborah asked Susan and Laney to meet with her and Detective Brody at a local diner. Deborah didn't want to break the news to him alone that Laney could find nothing in the Temple records, and she was hoping that with Susan and Laney's experience, perhaps they all might be able to come up with another idea.

"I was so sure this would be it," Detective Brody told them, sounding more than a little despondent upon learning that the funds all seemed to be intact.

"So I gathered from reading the newspapers," Susan said, with more than a touch of sarcasm.

"Don't be so critical," he responded. "You of all people know the pressure I'm under."

Detective Brody knew Susan King by reputation only: "A tough bitch," "Hard to beat in court," "A lesbian who eats men for breakfast." He couldn't help but be baffled by the obviously strong friendship between a lady like Deborah Katzman and the likes of Susan King.

"I've had my own share of handling newspaper reporters, Detective Brody. You are certainly right about that, but when you give out information based on wishful thinking and fantasy, you have to understand that you are bringing on your own demise."

Detective Brody reacted immediately to Susan's criticism, "A popular Rabbi gets shot, and we've got to find a murderer. It doesn't matter that there are no real leads, the public wants a murderer. Reporters are all over the place hounding me from morning to night to find a murderer. What am I supposed to do? I tell them I don't have anything, and they think, 'Oh, here we taxpayers are paying this bastard's salary and he's too lazy to do his job.' So I give them some tidbits here and there, so they know I'm not sitting in the office playing poker all day. I hope that I'll get lucky and things will fall into place. So far it hasn't happened."

Susan rolled her eyes at Deborah.

Deborah was beginning to feel uncomfortable due to the tension between Susan King and Detective Brody. Perhaps bringing them together in this way had not been a good idea. She had no idea there would be this kind of a personality clash between them. She looked up and caught sight of Carl walking through the swinging doors. He had also wanted to be part of this important brainstorming session, but wasn't certain he would be finished at the hospital on time. At the mere sight of him Deborah almost jumped for joy, right out of her seat.

"Am I happy to see you," Detective Brody quipped as Carl approached the table. "These lovely ladies were really ganging up on me."

"Women. We're women," Laney Baer corrected him. Deborah smiled at Carl.

"There have to be some clues," Susan replied. "I've told Deborah what I think and I'll repeat it again here: this is a crime of great passion. This Rabbi was shot up close, from what I understand. The way I see it, someone walked up to him, looked him in the eye, gave him an earful on whatever it was that engendered such strong emotions, maybe even cursed him out a bit, and then they shot him. I doubt that this had anything to do with money, although it is possible that money is peripherally involved in some way. But this is a Rabbi we're dealing with here, and it was an inside job, not a drive-by shooting by some lunatic. I just know that this has to do with love or hate, or perhaps both."

"Well," Deborah began, "I've been thinking about where to go from here. Leon recently told me that there is little that goes on at Beth Torah that he doesn't know about. I am reasonably sure that's true. We do know for sure that he knew something about the ledger book. We know that he tried to divert attention away from himself by starting a rumor about the Rabbi."

"Leon can be malicious, Deb, and that might be all there is to it," Carl interrupted.

"Yes, he can be malicious, but somehow I am reasonably sure that there is more to it than that. I just don't know what," Deborah replied. "I doubt that he's the murderer, but I'm willing to bet that he has a good idea of who is."

"Not from what he says," Detective Brody spoke up.

"Since when do we believe everything someone says?" Susan quickly added. "Can't you pick him up and try a little strong arm?"

"Excuse me," Detective Brody said, sarcastically. "Is this Susan King, the great civil libertarian I hear speaking? What's the matter, you think it's only women and homosexuals who have civil rights? You think maybe I should bring someone in for questioning without any evidence of wrong-doing? I do that and the next thing I know you or one of your partners will be representing him in his lawsuit against the local government and I'll be out of a job."

"Not everything has to be done officially, Detective. There are ways to do it and it's done every day of the week—you and I both know that," Susan said, clearly annoyed.

"No, not in a case as high profile as this one is. Everything I do is under scrutiny. I can't bring someone in for questioning without it being on the evening news, so if I bring him in, I'd damn well better have a good reason. If there was money missing from a fund, he's the administrator, then there's a reason. Now, there's no reason. Can't be done."

Laney had been sitting quietly, taking in all that was being said. "If you're the president of the congregation, Deborah, maybe you can go talk to him, kind of confront him with the idea that he is in some way involved with your Rabbi's murder, speaking just as the president, of course, and see how he reacts."

There were a few seconds of silence while everyone digested the logic of what she had to say.

"That's not a bad idea," Carl said. "You and I can go talk to him to-gether. Tell him that we think he knows something and see how he reacts."

"Of course, this could be dangerous, because if he has murdered once, he might not hesitate to murder again," Laney continued.

"No, I don't think so," Susan offered. "I feel strongly about my crime of passion theory. The person who did this in all likelihood might never hurt another human being. They killed to avenge themselves, to quiet the storm that was raging within them. With the Rabbi dead, the rage is gone. They might feel some guilt, but no rage."

"Your theory is a logical one," Detective Brody grudgingly admitted, "and something of that sort has crossed my mind as well, but there are times when a person has to continue murdering simply to cover up the first murder." The detective turned abruptly to Deborah and Carl, "Would you two be willing to record your conversation? If you go in with a wire, we can be monitoring what's going on, so if it becomes a dangerous situation, police officers can be on the scene relatively quickly; I can have a warrant prepared and ready."

Deborah and Carl looked at each other and grinned.

"My God," Deborah laughed out loud, "I'll be just like Dick Tracy, equipped with radio devices and all. This is too much. I think, though, I will have to go see him alone. If I'm talking to him as the president of the synagogue, I really can't have anyone with me."

"You've heard of an ounce of prevention, Deborah," Susan said. "Maybe you can come up with a reason for seeing him together with Carl."

"No, I don't think so. This is my job, not Carl's." Carl's facial expression and body language clearly showed his concern. Although she strongly believed that she had to see Leon by herself, she couldn't help but wonder if in the past she would have found some way to handle this together with Carl, that is, before Jonathan Levy's death. "Tell me, is the listening device in my shoe or a fountain pen?" she asked, attempting to lighten her husband's mood.

"Nothing that dramatic," the detective answered. "Probably a simple mike in your bra will do, but I'll leave that decision to the technicians."

"I hope we don't regret this whole scheme," Carl mumbled, but not loud enough for even Deborah to hear him.

"We'll be fine. Leon would never hurt me, of that I'm quite positive," Deborah answered with assurance. "Besides, if Susan's theory that this is a crime of passion is correct, we can be sure Leon is innocent—he's the least-passionate individual I've ever known."

"But you said you think he may have some idea of who is guilty," Susan said.

"If I were a betting person, I'd bet that he does know a lot more than he's told us," Deborah answered.

The evening newspaper headline read: "Police Hit Dead End in Finding Clues to Rabbi's Murder."

Deborah called Leon. She wanted to meet with him the following evening at five o'clock, after the rest of the synagogue staff had left the building for the day.

"Is there something wrong?" he asked.

"I just want to speak to you about a few things."

"Like what?"

"If I wanted to go over this on the telephone, Leon, I wouldn't be asking to come in and see you. I'm the president of the congregation. I have a few things to speak to you about. Isn't that enough?"

"You want me to stay late to meet with you, and you're not even going to tell me about what? That doesn't seem very fair."

Deborah found Leon more irritating than usual. "Since I don't want to be concerned about your repeating any part of what I have to say to you to one of our congregants, I think I'd rather keep all of what I have to say private until I see you."

"There's nothing wrong with my speaking to congregants. I'm supposed to speak to congregants. That's my job. I'm the administrator, remember?"

"I remember, Leon. But I choose not to talk about this over the telephone. We can continue this conversation when I get there tomorrow."

"Sure. But if I were being paid for overtime you wouldn't be asking me to stay past five o'clock for some BS reason like this."

"And I'm not paid at all for this wonderful job that I have, so let's just stop the BS. I promise I won't keep you very long."

Leon Feldman was angry. It was bad enough having to deal with a woman as president, but to make matters worse he had yet to get a handle on where Deborah Katzman was coming from, what her agenda might be. Over the years, when a new president got elected Leon would know what he was getting into. In the past it had always been somebody who came up the ranks over a period of time, so he'd have an opportunity to work with them on various projects, get to know how they thought. He would know their style, their strengths and weaknesses, and he would learn how to barter for those things that were important to him, but Deborah Katzman had arrived on the scene from out of nowhere. Even Rabbi Levinson had his own problems with her before he died. After all these months Leon still couldn't figure her out, and she made him squirm like no other president before her.

Leon Feldman did know that Deborah Katzman was always busy and she rarely wasted time. She wouldn't be asking him to stay late for some flimsy reason, but he didn't know what it was. He suspected it might have something to do with the Rabbi's death. He remembered the offhand remark he had passed to Deborah after Rochelle's faggot son died, but so what? He wanted her to know that he knew everything that went on in the synagogue, what she was missing by not trusting him.

Leon Feldman knew what his job was all about: he was paid to know everything that went on in the community that could possibly affect the synagogue. Every other president before Deborah Katzman had eventually come to understand what an asset he could be to them. With him on their side, the president had nothing to worry about. He always saw to it that they knew about any griping within the congregation so the president could contact whoever was involved and cover his ass. He would tell them who was pregnant, who was sick, who was getting divorced, who was having an affair—whatever the situation, he was the man to keep the president in touch with what was happening. Eventually every president realized what he could do for them. Sure, there were some he had worked with better than others over the years, but that had never mattered much because one thing was certain: like the sun that rose in the morning and the stars that brightened the night, every two to three years there was a new president of Beth Torah. If Leon didn't like the one that was there, he just had to tough it out and eventually someone else moved up the ranks, ready to play ball.

Rabbi Levinson had always appreciated Leon's talents and his assistance. Leon also kept Rabbi Levinson informed of what was going on in the personal lives of Beth Torah's congregants. If the Rabbi wasn't around, Leon himself would write letters under the Rabbi's name applauding some accomplishment or another, wishing them *mazel tov* or whatever else was appropriate for the moment. Even the Rabbi's great ability to fundraise was due primarily to he, Leon Feldman, pointing out members of the congregation who were on their way up the ladder in business or elated over one thing or another that made them ripe for a donation. Over the years he had built up a network of resources that allowed him to have his eyes and ears into the Beth Torah community so uniquely that this alone made him indispensable as the administrator.

Deborah Katzman had been the only president not to appreciate him. Had she at last come to realize his worth? Is that why she was coming to see him? If she was coming to probe him on who murdered the Rabbi, well, she was too late for that. He had made up his mind to keep out of this mess.

This could only cause him problems, and he was getting too old for this shit. Maybe if he was lucky she wanted to talk about their declining membership or something else rather innocuous. Maybe if he was real lucky Deborah Katzman, Esquire would quit at the end of her first year in office.

Certainly this position can't be much fun for her since the Rabbi's death.

Deborah drove into Beth Torah's parking lot feeling almost giddy. Carl was sitting with Detective Brody and two undercover police officers in a van designed to look like a telephone repair vehicle parked half a block away from the synagogue. One of the police officers was a middle-aged man, the other a younger woman who had helped Deborah hook the microphone into her bra. There was an unmarked police car in front of the building, with two men ready to run to her rescue should it become necessary. As an extra precaution, Detective Brody had also seen to it that there was a tap put on all the telephones in the synagogue.

"We should have a code word or phrase you can use, in case you feel you're in danger," Detective Brody commented.

"How about 'God help us?'" Deborah suggested.

"Not bad, given the situation," the detective answered.

"Well, I think I can work that into a sentence without too much trouble. And the word 'help' might be an extra clue for you to tune into."

"As long as you're not confusing us with God, there'll be no problem. We try to be competent, but we don't perform miracles."

"How disappointing," Deborah smiled.

Deborah and Detective Brody might have been comfortable bantering back and forth, but Carl was clearly unhappy about her going in to see Leon Feldman alone.

"This could be dangerous. I want to go with you," he demanded once again.

"No. If any purpose is going to be served at all, I have to do it alone. I can't begin to imagine Leon speaking to the both of us. But don't worry, he's not dangerous—I'm sure of that. Anyhow, this is my job, not yours."

They both knew to what she was making reference, but Carl decided to let the remark go by rather than reopen a still-sensitive wound. Instead he said, "A few days ago you thought he was guilty, now you're telling me he's not dangerous."

"Well, I thought he might have stolen synagogue funds. I still think he's capable of something like that, but his murdering the Rabbi never made much sense to me. The Rabbi was his ally. Without Rabbi Levinson he might not even have a job."

"Unless the Rabbi knew something about him that he chose not to have other people find out."

"I don't think so," Deborah insisted. "He's a cynic, he's not a particularly caring individual, and he's a general pain in the butt. I don't like him and I don't want to be his friend, but I don't think he's a murderer."

Deborah wondered if there was something lacking in her makeup that allowed her to be so nonchalant in a situation that was causing those around her to feel so tense. Perhaps surviving the Nazis made everything else that would ever happen in her lifetime seem trivial by comparison. Deborah could feel the hard microphone tucked under the wire of her bra; it was rubbing against her, irritating her sensitive skin, a constant reminder of the mission to be accomplished, but she had little apprehension over what was about to happen. To the contrary, Deborah felt much like an adolescent schoolgirl on an extraordinary adventure. Her adrenaline was rushing.

Deborah arrived at the synagogue right on time. Leon Feldman was sitting at his desk, waiting for her. He stood up as she walked into his office.

"Hi, Leon. I'm sorry about keeping you late. I got here as soon as I could."

"It's all right," he mumbled, impatiently waiting to find out what she was up to.

Although she had given it a lot of thought, Deborah had not practiced or memorized what she would say upon meeting with Leon. She wanted to be certain that what she had to say wouldn't sound rehearsed. She treated the situation just as she would an oral argument in court: she had a clear list in her head of ideas and points to be made, but would wait for the situation to unfold before deciding the best way to get them across. Leon was clearly not going to make this easy by cooperating.

"I was surprised, Leon, when you told me that you knew about Jonathan Levy's death. I didn't think Rochelle had told anyone."

Deborah noticed Leon's body stiffen as she spoke. Body language was worth a thousand words.

"I have my sources," Leon answered curtly.

"You obviously do. You've been here a long time and you know a lot of people."

Leon stared at her without commenting.

Damn him for being so obstinate, Deborah thought. She would have to shock him into some sort of reaction.

"Tell me, Leon, how did you know the Rabbi had a ledger book where he was keeping track of somebody's debt?"

Leon's face was turning red and he was clearly angry. He moved forward in his chair. "I don't know what you're talking about," he replied.

Deborah smiled, realizing she had the upper hand for the moment. "Of course you do. I know that you mentioned the ledger book to several people in the congregation."

"Are you talking about that absurd rumor about the Rabbi having a bookie or some such thing?"

"I also have my sources, Leon, and while all rumors take on a life of their own, I am quite certain that this particular rumor originated with you. What I want to know is why, and how you knew."

"I didn't start any rumors. I would never speak against the Rabbi. He was my friend. This is not about synagogue business, and I am going home."

"You can go wherever you want, but then I intend to go to Detective Brody with what I know."

"You don't know anything."

"I know that you're the only one in the synagogue who knew that the Rabbi was keeping track of some sort of payment in this ledger book. If you're the only one who knew about it, then it must involve you in some way. Maybe it was you who was repaying the Rabbi for who knows what? Maybe you missed a payment or two and got nervous and . . ." Deborah let her voice trail off.

"You're crazy," Leon shouted, jumping out of his chair.

"Maybe I am, but unless you tell me what you know, I am going to go to the police. Whether you realize it or not, Detective Brody is under a lot of pressure and they need to find a body to pin this on. Joyce Kaplan is quite positive that the police will arrest anyone just to get the public off their backs."

"Joyce Kaplan is a jackass!" Leon exclaimed out loud, but to himself he thought, *Of course, that blabbermouth bitch is the one who caused this mess.* He should have planted the seed with Rita; she would have just repeated it without bothering to worry about it being true or not. "What does Joyce Kaplan know? They have nothing to arrest me for. This is ridiculous," Leon rambled on.

"Fine. Then you go home, I'll call Detective Brody, and we'll see what happens from there."

Deborah was calm and collected. Leon's left eye was twitching.

"Why are you doing this? I didn't kill the Rabbi. Is that what you think? I didn't do it. What do you want from me?"

"I want you to tell me what you know. If you didn't kill the Rabbi, you yourself told me that very little goes on around here that you don't know about. I want to know about the ledger book, and I want to know everything you know about the murder."

"Why are you linking the ledger book together with the murder? What makes you think one thing has something to do with the other?"

"I'm not here to play games, Leon. Tell me what you know.

"I'll tell you only one thing, and then I'm going home," Leon announced in a stern voice.

"I'm waiting," Deborah stood her ground.

"I'm going to tell you to go see your friend Rochelle. Talk to her the way you did to me. See what she has to say to you."

"What does Rochelle have to do with this?"

"That's all I'm telling you. Now you're on your own. And since this is my office, I'd like you to leave."

Deborah was caught off guard. Was he telling her that Rochelle was involved with this ledger book or was he telling her that Rochelle murdered the Rabbi? She found herself without words. "Okay, I'll go to see Rochelle, but then I'm going to see Detective Brody."

"You do whatever it is you have to do, but do it out of my office. Goodbye."

Deborah turned around and walked briskly toward the parking lot exit. She was shocked at the mention of Rochelle's name, but felt quite vindicated. Clearly Leon was not about to harm her in any way and clearly he knew more than he had been willing to say prior to this moment in time.

As soon as Deborah was safely out of the building, Leon, unaware of the tap on his telephone, called Rochelle.

"Deborah Katzman came to see me about the ledger book. She thought I killed the Rabbi. She was threatening to turn me over to that detective who's been hanging around."

"So what did you tell her?"

"I told her to go see you."

"How could you do that to me, Leon? You promised."

"I didn't tell her anything. I just sent her to see you. You can tell her whatever you want. I can't afford to take any heat for you or anyone else. I've had about enough shit for one day and I'm going home. Good night!"

Chapter Twenty-Three

April 1993

As previously planned, Deborah met with Detective Brody and Carl in the back of Waldbaum's Supermarket.

"Rochelle." Carl was visibly shaken; he spoke barely in a whisper. "How could Rochelle have anything to do with this?"

"I'm going to drive over and speak to her now," Deborah said, ignoring his comment. "With or without this mike digging into my boobs, I'm going to see Rochelle."

"I certainly can go with you to see Rochelle," Carl asserted. "She and I have become quite close over the last few months. She trusts me."

"Of course, she knows Deborah is coming, she's been warned," Detective Brody interjected.

"How do you know that?" Deborah asked.

"Remember, we have a tap on the phone. Leon called her the minute you left the office."

"What did he say?"

"Nothing too incriminating, unfortunately. He basically just told her you were coming and she was on her own. About what, now, he wasn't kind enough to say."

"I was hoping Leon was just trying to buy time or something. I hate the thought that Rochelle is involved in this in any way at all." Deborah looked directly at Carl as she spoke.

"She isn't. She can't be," Carl insisted.

"Some murderers are very sympathetic characters, you know," Detective Brody proclaimed.

"Rochelle is no murderer," Carl said, his teeth clenched tightly together.

"Why don't we go and try to find out?" Deborah took Carl's hand and led him towards their car.

"Remember," Detective Brody shouted after them, "she doesn't know that you know that she knows you're coming . . . I think that makes some sense."

Carl drove much faster than usual and Deborah was nervous.

"Take it easy. One minute later is not going to make too much of a difference."

"I've got the MD plates and the police are right behind us. There's no problem."

"The problem is not the cops; you're driving too fast for me and you're making me crazy."

"Okay, okay," Carl slowed down to the speed limit.

"Thank you."

"Rochelle is not a murderer, Deb. I know she's not."

"You don't have to convince me because under normal circumstances I would be agreeing with you."

"Just because that slimeball Leon Feldman points to her, that doesn't make everything he says true."

"Actually, Leon didn't say she was the murderer. He just told me to speak to her, and that's what we're doing. Let's wait and see what she has to say."

As they drove up the circular driveway Deborah noticed the curtains parted just the slightest bit. "She's at the window, waiting for us."

"I hate this," Carl said, despondent over the prospect that Rochelle Levy was involved in the murder. "What are we going to say to her?"

Deborah watched the curtains fall back into place. "She's expecting us and she knows why we're here. I think we ought to tell her the truth, there's no point beating around the bush."

"Tell her that there's a tap on Leon's telephone?"

"Of course not. Just tell her why we're here."

"You do the talking. I'll follow your lead."

"Fine," smiled Deborah, pleased to be in charge of her husband for a change.

Rochelle greeted them at the door. "How nice to see you both," she lied. "Come in."

Deborah and Carl each gave her a peck on the cheek before entering. Deborah still had the microphone buried in her bra. She wondered if the truck had followed them over. She had been so involved in her conversation with Carl that she had forgotten to notice.

"Can I get you some coffee?" Rochelle asked.

"No, thank you," they both replied.

They sat down in the living room, a huge room with two windowed walls and a cathedral ceiling.

"Rochelle, you know that I'm a very direct person, and I don't care to play games with you. We're here because Leon suggested we come to see you," Deborah said without emotion.

"Whatever for?" she answered, clearly behaving as boldly as she could under the circumstances.

"I'm not sure. I was speaking to Leon about a ledger book that the Rabbi was keeping before he was murdered. We think this may have something to do with why he was murdered."

The expression on Rochelle's face quickly changed to one of horror. There was a moment of silence while she obviously contemplated what to say next. "Look, I can tell you about the ledger book, but that has nothing to do with the Rabbi's murder. It's completely separate. You've got to believe me."

"Of course we believe you, Rochelle," said Carl, sounding very sympathetic. Deborah glared at him.

"Why don't you tell us what you do know? Tell us about the ledger book," Deborah suggested.

"When Jonny was sick I wanted him to be as comfortable as possible. Harry wouldn't let him stay at the house. He was angry with Jonny, and Jonny didn't have enough money to live in his apartment. Disability didn't cover enough of his expenses. He needed constant care and I couldn't always be there, so I borrowed money from the Sisterhood bank account to pay for nurses.

"I was afraid to tell Harry what I was doing," Rochelle continued. "Harry was not the man I've known all these years, he was like a crazed stranger. It was as though someone else was living in his body. He refused to let me even mention Jonny's name, he was so upset about what was going on. I needed money for Jonny and I just couldn't go to Harry. I had nowhere else to turn."

Deborah suddenly realized that she had never given any of the Sisterhood accounts to Laney to review, she had only given her the synagogue fund accounts. That's why Laney didn't find any money missing. "You have no money in your own name?" Deborah asked in disbelief.

"Everything we have is in joint accounts. Usually Harry never asks me about what I spend, but there's no way I could have taken thousands of dollars out of the bank for Jonny's medical expenses without his wanting to know what I was doing with the money. I didn't want to make things worse with him, and Jonny needed help." Rochelle began to weep. "I'm a mother, what could I do?"

"Even if Harry was angry, how could you think he would have wanted to let Jonny suffer rather than make him comfortable?" Deborah was very skeptical about what Rochelle was telling her.

"You don't understand how people react to AIDS," Carl interrupted before Rochelle could answer. He got up and sat next to Rochelle on the couch, handing her a handkerchief from his pocket.

Deborah glared at him again, this time for his intrusion into her probing of Rochelle, but she went on as though nothing had happened. "So, you took money. Then what?"

"I didn't take money, I borrowed money," Rochelle corrected her. "And I was feeling very guilty about what I had done. So when Leon noticed that there was money missing from the Sisterhood account, and he called me, I felt I had to tell him the truth. I didn't know what else to do. Leon told the Rabbi what happened and the Rabbi worked out a plan where I was paying the money back. That was about it.

"I didn't kill the Rabbi, I swear to you, I didn't. He was helping me. Why would I kill him?"

"Of course, you didn't," Carl said, still comforting her.

"How much money do you owe Sisterhood?" Deborah asked.

"I still owe about nine thousand, and that amount varies a little bit, depending on the interest. I was paying the money back with one percent more interest than we would have gotten at the bank. That was Rabbi Levinson's suggestion. He said that would make it okay. No one was being hurt and I was helping Sisterhood by seeing to it that they earned more money than they would in the bank."

"He really had no right to do that, you know. These were not his private funds, but in a way I'm glad he was there for you and Jonny."

"Oh, he wasn't there for Jonny, if that's what you think. He wouldn't go see him."

"You asked him to see Jonny?" Deborah recalled that previously Rochelle denied ever discussing Jonny with Rabbi Levinson.

"Of course I asked him to see Jonny. He was our Rabbi. You just don't understand Deborah, AIDS is like the biblical leprosy. The Rabbi told me that Jonny was getting what he deserved. This was God's revenge for his homosexuality, but he was willing to help me, because I was a good person." Rochelle's voice cracked; she spoke with such emotion that it was painful to listen to her.

"Maybe I don't understand," Deborah whispered, still trying to sort out everything Rochelle had told them.

"Listen, Rochelle," Carl said, finding Rochelle's pain too much to endure, "We'll pay off the Sisterhood fund for you, and you can pay us back."

Deborah looked at him, flabbergasted at what he said.

"Right, Deb?" he asked, "We can lend Rochelle the money. We don't want to see her have a police record for something like this."

"I don't know, Carl, I think we have to talk about all of this," Deborah responded. She looked at Rochelle, "So, tell me, Rochelle, who do you think killed the Rabbi?"

"I don't know. I don't know who killed the Rabbi." Rochelle was staring down at her shoes.

Rochelle was avoiding eye contact. Deborah asked, "Do you think Leon killed the Rabbi?"

"I don't know," she answered, "but I don't think so. Why would he kill the Rabbi? They were friends." Rochelle continued to stare at her shoes.

"I'm sorry to tell you this, Rochelle, but I think that Detective Brody is going to want to question you further," Deborah said, waiting for Rochelle's reaction.

After a moment of silence, Deborah turned to her husband. "Carl, I would really like to speak to Rochelle alone."

Carl frowned, but he understood from the stern look on Deborah's face that he'd better go along with whatever it was she was doing.

Rochelle was frightened.

Good cop, bad cop, Deborah thought. *Maybe this can all work to our advantage after all.*

"Why don't you wait for me in the car?" Deborah said to her husband. "I won't be long."

Carl got up reluctantly, he winked at Rochelle, and left without saying anything further.

"Rochelle, I'm sorry to have to do this," Deborah said. "I do feel for you, and all that you've been through, but I couldn't speak with Carl around. Carl's compassion makes him a wonderful doctor, but he's just too involved with your situation to be objective. Personally, I think that you have a lot more to say than you have told us."

"I don't! I don't!" she sobbed.

Passion, Deborah could hear Susan King's voice pounding in her ear, *A crime of passion, someone who might never murder again.*

Once again Deborah felt a heaviness surrounding her that no words could describe, the same sensation she had experienced that day in the kitchen when she was speaking to Detective Brody and Carl, and again at Rabbi Levinson's grave. She didn't know if it was a manifestation of her own fear or if Rabbi Levinson was here with her, prodding her on.

"Rochelle," Deborah said very softly, "did you kill the Rabbi?"

Suddenly, Harry Levy appeared from nowhere. "Leave her alone. She didn't do anything." Obviously, he had been listening to everything that had gone on.

"Harry, don't," Rochelle cried out.

"It's all right, Rochelle, I can't live with this. I have no life anymore anyway. I deserve to die. My only son is dead and I didn't even have the courage to speak to him before he died." Harry turned towards Deborah and quietly said, "Rochelle would never do anything wrong. I killed the Rabbi."

Deborah's body physically shook, as though somebody had punched her. "You killed the Rabbi?" she gasped.

"The man deserved to die," Harry's voice trembled as he spoke. "I went to see him for help. I couldn't live with myself for the way Jonny turned out. He was my son. I wanted to be there for him, but I was ashamed. I wanted to help him, but I couldn't bring myself to help him. I hated him for what he was, but I loved him because he was my son. I went to my Rabbi for help and do you know what he told me?" Harry was hysterical; he was waving his fists frantically in the air; it was difficult to understand him as he spoke.

Deborah was paralyzed with fear. All she could do was nod in Harry's direction. Rabbi, she thought, if you're here now, I hope you're protecting me.

"He told me that it was my fault. That I had spent too much time working and making money and not enough time with my son. He told me that God was punishing both of us. He was punishing Jonny for being homosexual and he was punishing me for not being a good father. Can you imagine a Rabbi saying such a thing?"

Rochelle was crying. "No one would have found out. You didn't have to tell," she sobbed.

Suddenly there was a lot of noise, the front door flew open and Detective Brody burst into the house, followed by the middle-aged male and young female officers who had been in the truck. Carl was right behind them. He ran over and put his arm around Deborah's shoulders. Deborah buried her face into his shoulder and began to weep. The detectives were approaching Harry.

"Thank God it's over. Thank God it's over," Harry kept repeating.

"First my son, now my husband," Rochelle cried. "I'll be all alone. I can't live. You shouldn't have told them, Harry. No one would have known. No one would have known," she said over and over again.

Carl and Deborah walked over to try and comfort her. Deborah reached into her purse and pulled out a notebook. She wrote out Susan King's phone number and handed it to Rochelle. "Susan King is a criminal attorney, if anything can be done at all, she's the one to do it for you."

Rochelle nodded and continued sobbing.

The detectives led Harry out the front door.

Newspaper headlines throughout New York read: "Synagogue Member Confesses to Rabbi's Murder in Crime of Passion, Community in Mourning Once Again!"

Chapter Twenty-Four

June 1993

D eborah called her mother to see what was happening.
"Ben finished chemo today," her mother told her. "Things look good for the time being. We'll have to wait and see what happens."

"That's great, Mom. What about his children?"

"What about them? There's never going to be a love fest between us, but at least now they know for sure that I exist. Previously, they may have suspected, but they didn't know. In their hearts they have to understand that Ben needed some real companionship."

Deborah sighed, "I've learned a lot lately about emotions and passion and what those things can do to you. There's not necessarily any logic involved. If they see Ben as having betrayed their own mother, then that's the way they look at things. However, maybe with some time to think, they'll come to terms with it."

"I hope they do for Ben's sake. He could use some peace of mind," Brina answered. "We're going to go out with Uncle Jake and Aunt Rose over the weekend to celebrate—an end-of-chemo party, you might say."

"That sounds like something worth celebrating."

❧

The Rabbi's Search Committee had interviewed and reinterviewed ten Rabbis before narrowing their options down to Rabbi Gold or Rabbi Berger. There was no one left to interview. It was time to meet to decide exactly who Rabbi Levinson's replacement would be.

Deborah had spoken with representatives of each faction in the synagogue separately regarding the various rabbinical applicants for the job. She had met twice with representatives of the Young Couple's Club.

"We like Rabbi Berger," the YCC representatives had told her, but we believe that Simmy wants Rabbi Gold. Rabbi Gold is from South Africa and he's very traditional in his thinking."

Deborah agreed with their assessment of the situation. Brotherhood, indeed, was enthusiastic about Rabbi Gold, but she too felt that Rabbi Berger would be better for the congregation as a whole.

Deborah had investigated Rabbi Berger's background very thoroughly. Rabbi Berger had three daughters, no sons. His oldest daughter had run the junior congregation services at his last synagogue. She had also been a regular attendee at the daily *minyan*. She spoke about wanting to be a Rabbi herself. Both men were distinguished rabbis, worthy of a congregation like Beth Torah, but Rabbi Berger undoubtedly was more accepting of change, and Beth Torah needed peace.

The night of the Search Committee meeting Deborah arrived at the synagogue early and waited in her car until she saw Simmy Monash drive up. She opened the car door and jumped out, calling to him. He smiled at her.

"Hello, Simmy," she shouted, walking towards him. He waited for her to catch up.

"This is really great," Deborah said enthusiastically, "I think we're all in agreement that Rabbi Gold is the candidate of choice."

"Is that so?" Simmy sounded surprised.

"Oh, yes. The rumor is that the Brotherhood is in favor of him, as you must know since you're their representative, and I think the YCC wants him because he is a very strong advocate of human rights."

"I didn't know that," Simmy answered, "but I speak for Brotherhood, so you shouldn't be paying attention to rumors."

Deborah continued. Knowing how obstinate Simmy could be, she hoped that he would be contrary enough to reject Rabbi Gold if he believed the YCC was promoting him. "Rabbi Gold took a strong anti-apartheid stand when he was in South Africa. He believes in equality for all people," Deborah went on, "and the YCC is hoping that will mean women too."

"I see," Simmy said, listening carefully. "Well, we'll have to see about all of this."

Barry called the meeting to order. "Since we have narrowed this down to Rabbi Berger and Rabbi Gold, two very capable Rabbis, let's go around the table and see if we can come to some sort of consensus."

At Deborah's suggestion Barry agreed to call on the YCC last. He called first on the new, unanimously elected Sisterhood President, Sonia Levinson. "Rabbi Berger is a deeply religious man from a well-known rabbinical family. I think he should be our first choice, if we are lucky enough to get him. Rabbi Gold, of course, is also a wonderful Rabbi, but the man I think who could best fill my Saul's shoes is Rabbi Berger. They have similar backgrounds."

The next one to speak was Simmy Monash. "Rabbi Berger is a scholar," he said, smiling sadistically at Joyce Kaplan. "We need a scholar at Beth Torah, someone smart enough to get us through the terrible ordeal we've been through. The Brotherhood votes for Rabbi Berger."

Joyce looked at Deborah and kicked her under the table.

Barry nodded towards Joyce. "After much consideration, the YCC does not wish to be obstructionist. In the interests of keeping peace in our synagogue, we too will go along with both Sisterhood and Brotherhood and vote for Rabbi Berger." Joyce muffled a giggle, much like an adolescent schoolgirl.

Simmy Monash shouted victoriously, "Amen!"

Barry and Deborah grinned broadly at each other. Beth Torah, *The Synagogue*, the one they loved, was beginning a new day, and life indeed would go on after all.

"So, you must be feeling very proud of yourself," Carl replied upon hearing Deborah's interpretation of what had happened at the meeting. "You not only solved the Rabbi's murder, but you even managed to get unanimity on which Rabbi to hire. I was right, you were the best person for the job of president."

"Thank you, but I don't think I solved the Rabbi's murder."

"Of course you did. If not you, who do you think did it?"

"I think Rabbi Levinson led us in the right direction. I think he solved his own murder."

"Deborah, in all these years, your father, who was also murdered, never came to see you, but Rabbi Levinson did? It doesn't make any sense."

"It doesn't have to make sense, and you don't have to believe it. Maybe my father was out there protecting me. Maybe that's how come I arrived in England alive. I don't know, but what's important for me is that the Rabbi came to guide us. It makes sense to me. I felt his presence and I believe he steered me in the right direction."

"I'll take your word for it," Carl said, reaching out for her hand. After all these years of marriage, Carl Katzman knew that some things were best left unsaid.

The next morning, Deborah visited Rabbi Levinson's grave. The unveiling still had not yet taken place and the grave was still without a headstone. Deborah picked up some pebbles and laid them down on top of the dirt. "Well, Rabbi, I don't know if you actually spoke to me last time I was here or not, but if you did, thanks for your help. I guess now you can finally rest in peace."

The morning newspaper headline read: "Temple Prez Announces New Rabbi For Beth Torah."

"The synagogue's healing process can at last get underway," says Ms. Deborah Katzman, President of Beth Torah, commonly known as *The* Synagogue. "We look forward to welcoming Rabbi Berger into our community," Ms. Katzman declared.

CPSIA information can be obtained
at www.ICGtesting.com
Printed in the USA
BVHW041712120720
583553BV00014B/234

9 781725 267947